SOUTH

BILLIONAIRE RANCH - 2

VANESSA VALE

South by Vanessa Vale

Copyright © 2021 by Bridger Media

This is a work of fiction. Names, characters, places and incidents are the products of the author's imagination and used fictitiously. Any resemblance to actual persons, living or dead, businesses, companies, events or locales is entirely coincidental.

Cover design: Bridger Media

Cover graphic: Wander Aguiar Photography; Deposit Photos: designwest

GET A FREE VANESSA VALE BOOK!

Join Vanessa's mailing list to be the first to know of new releases, free books, special prices and other author giveaways.

http://freeromanceread.com

1

*S*OUTH

IT WAS her ass I saw first. Perfect. Lush like a peach. Wiggling as it stuck out of the fridge. I paused and stared because... I wasn't dead. I leaned against the mudroom doorway, crossed my arms and enjoyed the view. After a morning fighting with a piece of metal that wouldn't bend the way I wanted, this was a treat.

She was a treat. I hadn't seen the rest of her besides the way her jeans were molded, but so far, so good.

Hell, so far, incredible.

I'd hated this house for years, just now finally getting comfortable inside these walls that had seen too much when I was a kid. The view of a perfect ass was better. So much better.

One twitch of that perfection and I'm rock-hard. Like one stroke and I'd come kind of hard. A teenager who couldn't control his dick kind of hard.

She tugged out a glass shelf and set it in the sink filled with soapy water. Food items like mustard and milk were on the counter. Then she saw me. Gasped. She yanked the earbuds free and let them dangle by the cord.

Fuck, the rest of her... my dick swelled and spurted pre-cum. *Just like that.*

"God, you scared me," she panted, then offered me a shaky smile. One that said I'm not sure if I'm safe with you.

That voice. Soft, deep. Breathy. I imagined what it would sound like saying my name. *South. Yes, South! More.*

"Shit, you're beautiful," I told her, shifting in the hope my zipper wouldn't leave a permanent mark on my dick.

She really was beautiful. Maybe it was the artist in me that noticed, because she sure as hell was trying to hide it. Dark hair pulled back in a sloppy bun that hid its length. I could tell it would fall to at least the center of her back by the thickness. Slide over pink nipples.

Glasses hid her wide eyes, but I couldn't miss the chocolate color. No, aged whiskey. Deep and rich. She wore no makeup, but she didn't need it, especially the way a deep blush colored her cheeks.

I wanted to tug on that hair tie and let those thick locks cascade over her shoulders. Kiss those full lips. Yank off that loose t-shirt and see every inch she hid beneath. Not all that well because those hips were wide, that rack full and more than a handful. I'd surprised her and I was an ass for not apologizing—and for thinking so long with my dick.

"Beautiful?" She rolled her eyes. "I'm up to my arms in soap suds and smell like furniture polish. You get kicked by a horse or something?"

It seemed like it, looking at her. I'd never felt like this before. Never had a reaction so strongly. Oh, I'd had my fair share of women, but they'd fulfilled a need. Nothing more.

This? This was way fucking more than need. It was like something in me shifted. That I'd been waiting for this moment. For her.

She was young. Legal, definitely, but I had to wonder if she could buy herself a drink. No wonder I didn't know her. A small town meant knowing everyone and their business, but she'd probably been in elementary school when I went off to college. That meant I'd been waiting for her to be old enough to be mine. That was if she'd even grown up here.

Who was she?

I was going to find out. I was at the big house to see Jed. He would know. Since he got together with North, he knew everything that went on around here.

As I took a step closer, she held up her hand. "Stop right there."

I froze, then couldn't help but smile at this pint-sized woman bossing me around. In my sister's house. Hell, Jed could wait.

"What?" I asked. "I won't hurt you."

I needed her to know I might be a foot taller and probably a hundred pounds heavier, but I'd never do anything to harm her.

"Don't bring all that dirt in here," she said, looking me over. "You might be a hot cowboy, but you're going to make a mess."

I grinned. "*Hot cowboy*, huh?"

She rolled her eyes again, then pointed at me. "You don't need that fact pointed out. The dirt though..."

I took off my Stetson and looked down at myself. My white t-shirt had dirt stains, a small tear where I'd snagged the fabric on a sharp corner of my latest work. Metal was unforgiving and messy. My jeans had seen better days, the knees soiled from where I'd knelt on the floor of my studio to weld a section in place. My boots were dusty and worn. Clearly, I didn't look like one of the homeowners. While North was the only one who lived here now, I'd grown up in this mansion until I went off to college. She'd remained, stuck here with Macon, our father.

No, from what North's ex-assistant Julian had said, he wasn't our fucking father after all.

It didn't matter. This was Wainright Ranch and I was a Wainright. I belonged here.

Obviously, she didn't know that. I didn't know who she was, but reading the white script on the t-shirt over her perfect right tit, she worked for Nancy's Cleaning Service. She was one of the maids? If her last name wasn't Wainright, she worked here.

I might have been a billionaire, but I respected anyone who earned their living the hard way. Through hard work. Unlike Macon, who'd married it. He might've earned a hefty salary as CEO of Wainright Holdings, but the real cash had been our mother's.

"I'm a little dirty, huh?" I said, chagrined. As a sculptor, I never stayed clean on a project.

"Don't tell me North gets mad at you if there's a mess. Or a messy person interrupting you."

"North?" she asked, pushing her glasses up.

"Mad?" She looked surprised. "She's a sweetheart."

I opened my mouth to argue. My sister? The ice princess? At least *former* ice princess since her man Jed had thawed her? Since most of her stress died with Macon?

"Don't say anything otherwise," she added, giving me a stern librarian look through those glasses.

I frowned. "You afraid of being fired?" That wasn't going to happen. Although if I had my way, she wouldn't be working here long. I didn't know her dreams. Her plans. I doubted they were scrubbing someone else's fridge. I'd help her with them. See them come true.

"No. Her father passed away recently, and she's been through a lot. The entire family has. Just because they have money doesn't mean they don't have hardship."

I blinked. "You're right," I agreed, knowing the truth of her words firsthand. I only wasn't expecting her to say so.

She was defending North. And me. She didn't even know it. I liked her even more. I was used to women flinging themselves at me. At my money. I didn't look like a million bucks all the time like North. More like a *billion*. This place wasn't nicknamed Billionaire Ranch for nothing.

I lived in a simple farmhouse down the road,

refusing to live in this place. Worked with my hands sculpting metal from scrap to art. Lived off my commissions, never touching a dime of my trust. Sure, I ate the Wainright cook's food when I came over. I enjoyed the liquor cabinet from time to time. I rode the horses. On occasion, I even flew in the helicopter that was North's main commute to the office.

But I never wanted to be known for being South Wainright, billionaire.

I was just a man.

And I'd found my woman.

She didn't know it yet.

"All right, beautiful." I couldn't help the endearment. She was so fucking lovely. Inside and out. "I don't want to make more work for you." I crooked my finger. "Come over here."

"I really need to get back to my work." She thumbed over her shoulder toward the fridge.

"North's a sweetheart, you said. She'll understand you wanting to take a minute to talk to a hot cowboy."

She huffed out a laugh. "If I'd known it would go to your head, I'd never have said it."

"Too late."

Yeah, it was too fucking late for both of us.

"You're cute," she countered.

It was my turn to laugh. "Cute? Beautiful, I've never been called *cute* in my life."

Fucker. Dumbass. Pansy. Stupid. Macon had tossed all that out and I'd let it stick. For years. But I'd still gone to art school. Gotten away from his poison and lived my life. Made something of myself on my own. Proved him wrong. I just hadn't realized the price North paid for it until after the asshole had been dead and buried.

"You know what's cute?" I said, steering my thoughts back to what was important. *Her.* "That ass of yours. Now get it over here."

A pretty flush crept into her cheeks. I saw the interest in her eyes. The desire to obey. She thought I was more than hot. More than cute. I couldn't miss the hard points of her nipples through her t-shirt. I'd bet my latest commission she was wet for me.

She came over but not close enough. I reached out, snagged her hand in mine and pulled her so my chest almost bumped hers. I wanted her in my arms, my mouth on hers, to drag her into some barely-used room and learn what made her gasp my name, but I was smart enough not to come on too strong. If she could read my mind, she'd run away screaming. Good thing she couldn't.

Jed came into the kitchen from deep in the house.

For some reason, he liked to work at Macon's desk in that stuffy fucking office. The room had been filled with animal heads; conquests Macon had killed for sport. North and Jed had found a place to deal with the animals respectfully, so it wasn't like a horror flick going in there any longer.

She flushed and tried to take a step back seeing Jed, but I curled my fingers around her elbow.

"Be with you in a sec, Jed," I said, never taking my eyes off of her.

"Came to tell you I'm driving to Billings to get North. Too windy for the helicopter," he murmured. "I'll talk with you when I get back."

"Sure," I replied. "Got a phone, beautiful?"

She nodded as Jed's footsteps got quieter. We were alone again.

"Can I see it?"

"Why?" she asked, even while pulling it out of her jeans' pocket. She had a Band-Aid around the top of her pointer finger. I wasn't the only one who had rough hands. I didn't like the idea of her getting hurt, even something small that only required a simple covering.

"So I can put my number in there so you'll call me," I explained.

She handed it to me as she bit her lip. Yet she asked again, "Why?"

I leaned in so we were eye to eye. "Because I want to take you out. Get to know you. Kiss you."

She laughed again. "You just met me five minutes ago."

"Don't need more than that to know what I want. Besides, you just met me and handed me your phone. You feel it, too."

She looked up at me, her head tilted back because I was so much taller. Nodded.

Fuck, yes.

"But Jed—"

"Don't worry about Jed. We've done nothing wrong."

I texted myself from her cell and mine dinged from my pocket. Confident I wouldn't be without her for long, I handed hers back. Stroked a knuckle down her cheek. "I respect you have work to do. I'll let you get back to it. Text me."

I leaned down, brushed my lips against her forehead, then left, confident. As I turned around to leave —the meeting with Jed delayed—I grinned. I didn't even know her name, yet the woman was mine. I was leaving her now, but not for long.

2

M AISEY

I SWIPED at the steamy mirror in my tiny bathroom. Grabbing my glasses I'd left on the sink while I showered, I stared at myself and wondered what the guy saw in me. I took in my wet hair that clung to my neck and back. My plain eyes. Plain face. Everything about me was plain. Boring. Average.

Yet he'd called me beautiful.

I couldn't stop thinking about him. He'd scared the crap out of me, then rocked my world. And all we'd done was talk. I'd given him my phone as if under a spell. Maybe I had been. Still was, hours later.

I thought of his broad shoulders and the way his dirty t-shirt had been molded to them. The worn jeans that cupped... everything just right. But it had been his eyes that had pulled me in. The deepest blue. I wasn't used to being the focus of such intense scrutiny, instead usually ignored. He'd looked at me as if I was... everything. As if he'd been waiting for me.

It felt as if I'd been waiting for him. The guys I'd dated in the past, they'd been boys in comparison. Actually, they really had been boys. Mere high schoolers. After my sister's I-want-what-you-have attitude had ruined any chance at a boyfriend in high school, I'd eventually given up because she stole every one of them. Any hint of interest on my part and she took it. Especially after Tommy, the only guy I'd slept with. Once. Then she'd sunk her claws into him, and they'd done things together I still hadn't tried. Guys had always wanted her instead of me, even though we were identical.

She was the fun one. The wild one. She had the same plain hair and eyes and yet she wasn't *plain*.

I'd never stood a chance, especially since she saw sex as part of the conquest. I still wasn't sure if it was to prove she was better than me or solely because she liked new and shiny things. Maybe both. She was a narcissist through and through. She wasn't satisfied until she had what she wanted that was mine, then twisted it around so it was my fault she'd taken it from me. A homecoming date. A paycheck. My entire bank account.

But Paisley wasn't here. After what she'd done —*this time*—I cleared out in the middle of the night. Took whatever fit in my car and left. Ditched my phone for a cheap pay-in-cash model. Cut up my sole credit card—even though I'd be paying down the maxed-out balance she'd accrued for years. I paid the minimum on my student loans and was living hand to mouth.

If I had extra cash, it would go to the mammogram that was recommended. I set my fingers over my left breast, pressed on the spot where I'd found the small lump. I'd gone to the free clinic where the nurse had felt it too and told me to go to Billings or Bozeman for more tests. She'd said I was young and it was probably nothing. A fluid filled cyst.

Still, they were tests I couldn't afford thanks to Paisley since I didn't have insurance.

For the past two months, she didn't know where I was. I'd get enough to pay for the tests and try not to panic in the meantime. I could think of better things. Like the guy at the ranch. Knowing Paisley wasn't around had given me some confidence when I'd talked with him.

No one in town even knew I had an identical twin. So when Hot Cowboy—I didn't even know his name! —looked at me like he wanted to lick me like a melting ice cream cone, he wasn't mistaking me for Paisley.

It made no sense. Why me? I was a down-on-her-luck housecleaner. I was a college dropout, thanks to Paisley. I was broke, again thanks to Paisley. I had no idea how to date. How to be anything but... me. Average. Plain. I'd learned that didn't keep men.

I closed my eyes and sighed, then felt the flutters in my stomach again. He wanted me to call him. It was getting late. I'd thought about what I'd say, if he'd even answer as I cleaned the hell out of the fridge and completed the rest of the to-do list at the Wainright house.

The guy wanted to go out with me, and I didn't even know who he was. If he'd been hired by the Wainrights, he had to be an okay guy. And he was employed. That was a plus, even though whatever he did was a filthy job. Good thing I was a cleaner.

Gah!

It was insane, the attraction. How he made me feel. It had been instant. Like a switch had been turned on.

There had been a connection, something I couldn't explain, even with a guy who was probably a decade older. It wasn't like I lived cloistered in a convent. I saw men all the time. Hot men. Hot *cowboys,* but I'd never felt like this. It seemed as if when he left a part of me went with him.

I grabbed the tub of generic moisturizer and smeared some on my face.

I wanted to feel his finger stroking my cheek again. Other places, too. The guy had said *all* the right things. Made me feel special. Pretty, even, and I'd been up to my arms in fridge cleaning.

Who was he? Why had he come into the house? What was his job on the ranch? Something that had him working hard for those muscles. Something dirty. I hadn't missed the knicks and scratches on his hands. No fancy suits or manicures for him.

Paisley appreciated a sugar daddy, a trait she'd picked up from our mother. The life of luxury without actually working for it. Although living in a beat-up trailer with guy number... twenty wasn't luxury.

I didn't want that. I wanted a strong man to be there for me. To build a life based on hard work and love. Mutual respect and passion. Money was important, but it wasn't everything.

I was so tired of taking care of others.

I'd always been the reliable one, the sensible one. My father had left when we were two. My mother never held a job for long. Nothing steady and nothing that had ever paid more than minimum wage. She'd often quit whatever her latest job was because of some kind of sure thing to bring in quick cash. There'd been a whole list of *sure things* growing up, but none had ever fixed the broken part on the trailer's heater or paid the electric bill. I'd had to make a loaf of bread and peanut butter stretch by getting a job at fourteen.

Six years later, not much had changed. Mom was living in the trailer but with her latest boyfriend who was supposed to give her all kinds of shiny things, but instead moved in and mooched off her. Paisley had stolen from me, not just money but my chance for my degree. Needing cash, she went to my bank, withdrew my college money. Spent it on a trip to Mexico for herself and the Guy of the Week.

Mexico! I hadn't even been out of Montana.

It still made me furious thinking about how hard I'd worked—while going to school full time—to save up and she'd blown it at the beach. That had been what had pushed me to the edge, discovering I'd overdrafted on my account at the registrar's office. That they'd cancelled my enrollment. That was when I called her and she'd admitted to it by sending a photo of her tan lines.

Before she returned, I left. Cleared out before Mom could question, not that she was paying me much attention other than covering the electric bill. I'd moved to a tiny town three hours away in the hopes of starting over. Hoping Mom would have to figure out her own household bills and that Paisley would catch on that I wasn't her meal ticket any longer.

It didn't matter anyway. I had nothing left. Mom always took Paisley's side and Paisley took everything. I literally had nothing to give either of them. I had my clothes, a few trinkets and mementos. My beater car that was more rust than running. I worked. I read. I slept. I was a loner.

So the idea of a guy like Hot Cowboy all alpha and bossy crooking his finger made me hot. I'd crossed to him in the Wainright kitchen without thinking. Just... obeyed.

My nipples were hard beneath my towel. A few minutes with the guy and he affected me.

I went to the dresser and pulled out a t-shirt and leggings, then sat on my bed. The house was tiny. It was an old miner's shack or something with only one room with a bathroom. It had come furnished, was clean, cheap and safer than the trailer where I'd grown up.

Should I call him? Could I? I grabbed the phone I'd left on the bed, stared at my text display. Bit my lip.

Hot Cowboy was at the top. He'd texted himself one word: Beautiful.

I wasn't sure if he was sweet or sexy or too good to be true.

All I had to do was touch my screen. I took a deep breath, let it out. Tried to calm my nerves. It wasn't any use. He had me tied up in knots ever since I first laid eyes on him.

No. I couldn't do it. I couldn't call him. What if he'd changed his mind? What if he'd been messing with me? What if...

He really *was* too good to be true. We'd talked for five minutes. Maybe less. That was why he'd asked me out. He hadn't had enough time to know the real me. Become aware of all the baggage I had. That I wasn't experienced sexually like Paisley. No doubt he had needs, desires that ran as dark and dirty as he was. I couldn't give him that. I had no idea how.

Besides, being into a guy after knowing him for five minutes was something my mother would do. Become enamored, then reliant, without any kind of solid foundation. I didn't even know his name. I'd tried to be nothing like my mother and with one sly smile, I discovered just how weak I was. One crook of his finger and I'd gone to him as if under a spell.

Plugging the phone into the charger, I set it on the floor, then climbed in bed and turned off the light.

I didn't call. Because if I did and he'd changed his mind about how beautiful I was, how he wanted to go out with me, it would hurt. More than it did right now. Just like all the times my mother had been dumped.

These days, I had hope. Hope that I would never be like her. Never have my sister find me and fuck me over again. Hope that I could make something of myself if I didn't keep getting pulled down. That was all I clung to because that was all I had. Hope was the only thing my sister couldn't take from me.

Still, I fell asleep thinking of blue eyes and lethal smiles.

3

S OUTH

"You learned I'm Macon's son and waited until now to tell me?" I asked, crossing my arms over my chest so I didn't beat the shit out of Jed.

After twenty years with the FBI, he wasn't easily intimidated. He'd dealt with all kinds of bad shit, but fuck... I was actually Macon's son. I ran a hand over my face.

"You looked a little busy," he replied.

North was pulling ice cream from the freezer and turned. "With what?"

With a spoon in her hand and a half gallon of

Rocky Road and in sweats with thick fleece socks, she looked far from the ass-kicking CEO.

"I'm interested in one of the house cleaners," I told her.

North's blonde brows arched, but she didn't say anything, instead, peeled off the lid and dug into the dessert.

"Maisey," Jed clarified.

Maisey.

"She's nice," North said, eating a spoonful.

"She passed the usual employee background check," Jed told me.

"Good to know. Thanks," I replied. I'd never even considered having North's team of people look into women I was interested in before. Never considered it. I liked to discover all on my own.

The Wainright Ranch employed a lot of people and we'd always had the staff checked out as part of being hired. Jed had taken on the task since he was ridiculously protective of North. While I was hating the man right now, I couldn't knock how he took care of my sister.

Finally someone was.

"Let's skip my love life for a minute," I continued. "You're sure about the DNA test?"

Jed went to the counter and picked up a piece of

paper and handed it to me. I scanned the results of me as well as my siblings, North, East and West. I was a definite direct match to both Kitty Southforth Wain- right and Macon Wainright. "Only me."

North grabbed another spoon from the drawer and handed it to me, then set the ice cream on the counter in front of me. "Only you." She pointed her own spoon at the paper. "We all share Mom, but East, West and I share a different father."

"Who?"

She shrugged.

I didn't want the ice cream. I wanted something stronger, but I was driving home. There were enough bedrooms to crash here, but I hadn't spent the night under this roof since high school graduation. North had cleared out the place of all of Macon's things, but she couldn't rid it of the memories.

I sighed, jabbed the spoon into the carton. "I thought we were rid of Macon."

"We are," North insisted, setting her hand on my arm. "He's only a sperm donor. Nothing more."

"Why would mom get with him? I mean, she had to know he was gay. Right? You're older than me. He knew he wasn't the guy who knocked her up, unless she lied to him. It's not like they had DNA testing back then." I sighed, then continued. "We also thought he hated us because we weren't his. That makes sense, in a perverse way. But I was his. He hated us all the same."

She shrugged. "The answers went to the grave with them."

I ran a hand over my face. "Fuck."

It made no sense. If Macon was gay, why would he sleep with our mom? Did she threaten to divorce him if he didn't give her kids? If so, why didn't she just have an affair, which she probably did with North, East, and West. So if they didn't have sex to make North, then why to make me? Had Macon forced our mother? That made no sense either. He wasn't into women. And who *was* their father?

"You going to be okay?" Jed asked, tugging North into his side and wrapping an arm around her waist.

Eddie, North's dog, trotted in from the mud room and bumped up against my leg. I reached down and stroked his head. His fur was cold. He must've been outside. Boozer, Jed's mutt, followed right behind and got in on the scratches.

"I just wish it was over. These results only make me question more. Would you be psyched if the results were different and North had Macon's blood in her?" I asked him.

"I don't give a shit about any of that. It makes no difference to me," he replied.

North went up on her tiptoes and kissed his cheek.

"You can say that now since the results are in," I replied.

Jed gave me his even stare but said nothing.

There wasn't anything to say. I was stirring shit up because I was pissed.

"There's no known relations in the system to Macon Wainright," Jed said. "A distant cousin in Arkansas. He's in his seventies and hasn't come forward."

"Macon was gay. He liked dick. That's the best way not to get someone pregnant." Yeah, I was fucking grumpy.

"We've had three people say they're mom's kids, wanting some of the inheritance."

I stared, then laughed. The inheritance in question was Macon's money, not the Southforth fortune.

"Of course they did. Because they read about Macon—dear old dad—dying?"

North shrugged. "I doubt mom had seven kids."

"She wouldn't have left them." I'd been little when she'd died. Barely remembered her. Only the scent of her perfume and a pair of orange pants, which made no sense. But I remembered her love for me. Hugs or something that made me deep down know that she'd wanted me. And North and the twins. No way would she have given up kids.

North waved a hand. "DNA doesn't lie. Those people can say all they want, but none are a match. They're all out."

"Then there are the ones who will say they're Macon's kids."

I frowned. "Who the fuck would want to do that?" I was his kid and I didn't want to be.

"Swindlers," North said.

"Liars," I added. "Why do people have to be so shady?"

"Money," Jed replied.

"The bulk of the money was all Mom's. Macon couldn't touch it." They both knew this, but they weren't making sense.

"Macon wasn't in the poorhouse. Sure, he lived here." Jed circled his finger in the air to indicate Billionaire Ranch. "As you know, this was all your mom's though. He earned a hefty salary from Wainright Holdings. Investments. He was a rich man."

"That's why he stuck around," North said. "It has to be. I knew him the best. Power and money was all he lived for."

"Let me guess, all of his money is mine, right?"

"Right."

"The lawyers figured that out, then they can figure out how to donate it all. I don't want a dime of it." Was I stupid to turn down money when people worked their fingers to the bone trying to put food on the table? I had plenty of cash. Too fucking much. I'd give it to those in need. Macon would roll over in his grave giving it to the needy. Which made me wonder...

"Do you think Macon even knew I was his kid?" I asked.

North shrugged.

"Let it go," Jed advised.

"That's a hard fucking request," I told him.

"Go get the girl." He looked down at North, stroked her hair back. "I'm going to have mine."

Before they started kissing in front of me, I left. The cold night air was bracing, but I needed it. I didn't want to think of North having sex with Jed. Instead, I thought of *her*. The woman who was going to be mine. It warmed me more than my truck's heater ever could.

I just needed her to call me so I could make her mine. It was her sweetness, her innocence that drew me in. So different from all the vultures circling the Wainright name.

4

 OUTH

Me: You didn't call.

I STARED AT MY TEXT, waited for Maisey to reply. I felt like a teenage girl with her first crush. Next I'd be writing Beautiful on my papers with a little heart over the "i". I'd even paused in my work to give in and message her.

After talking to North and Jed, I'd gone home. Cranky as fuck.

Stuck with Macon as a father and impatient for a

woman to call me, both of which were out of my control. I'd spent a sleepless night angry Maisey was somewhere in the county, probably wearing something skimpy and sexy. Alone. I could have been in bed with her. *In her.*

Forgetting all about my tainted DNA.

My morning was spent in my studio working on my latest commission. Using my cutters and banging metal helped with my frustration, but it was lunchtime, and she still hadn't called.

Had I come on too strong? No, I'd seen the way she'd flushed. How her nipples had hardened. How she'd smiled. Bit her lip. Called me *hot cowboy.* She'd given me her phone instead of running away screaming.

She wanted me as much as I wanted her. I'd felt it. Seen it.

I knew it.

Little dots on my screen showed she was typing and I leaned against my kitchen counter to wait. My dick punched against my jeans once again. Fuck, it was uncomfortable. I groaned in frustration, set the phone down as I slid down the zipper to give my dick some room. I sighed, but there wouldn't be true relief yet.

I'd seen the eagerness to please in her eyes. Why was she only responding now that I texted her first? Why didn't she call?

Fuck, I was growing a pussy.

Leaving Maisey behind in North's kitchen had been hard. So had my dick. I'd gone straight home, hopped in the shower and rubbed one out. I'd barely gotten in a few good tugs before I spurted all over the tile, visions of her tight ass in my head. The idea of getting a good grip on it as I fucked her had finished me off with a rough groan.

It hadn't helped much because a day later my dick was *still* hard and I had a feeling it would be until I got inside her and made her mine officially.

I learned from Macon—my fucking father—that so much time had been wasted. It had taken him to up and die to discover the truth. While my brothers, sister, and I knew he'd been an asshole, he'd also been a liar. A cruel fuck who liked to play with people. Especially North.

What she'd finally shared with us... what she'd done... *fuck.* I wasn't sure if I'd ever get over it. He hadn't touched her, but he'd been ruthless with her. If he were still alive, I'd have killed him, buried him in the back forty where no one but the wildlife would ever find the body. Even now, just thinking about what he'd done, about the things North had yet to tell us...

He'd messed with me and my brothers, but North had sheltered us. Bargained for our freedom. I'd gone into art as I'd always wanted, regardless of the insults Macon had hurled at me as a kid. My long desire for art school and he'd made me feel less. Made my dreams seem worthless.

I'd made something of myself anyway. I'd rarely seen the man since I graduated high school, avoiding him just as East and West had. His heart attack while in bed with his lover—his *male* lover—had been our release from an invisible prison.

My artwork was well known. I had more commission requests than I could handle. Until Macon's death, all I'd done was work. I barely saw my siblings. He'd been gone since July and now we saw each other often enough. The truth had been revealed about what Macon had done and we were making up for lost time.

Which meant I saw the woman I wanted and I didn't want to waste a minute. I knew she was mine and a second apart was a second lost. She didn't feel the same way, obviously. I had to change that, but that wouldn't work unless she called me. Responded. The bubbles on the screen stopped and her message appeared.

> Beautiful: I can't.
> Me: Working?
> Beautiful: Yes, but I mean I won't.

I frowned. *Won't?* What the fuck?

> Me: Why not?
> Beautiful: It would never work.

It wouldn't work? I glanced down at my dick, outlined by my boxers. Oh, it worked.

> Me: Give me a chance. Give US a
> chance.

My thumbs were too big to type on such a small screen, but I had to get this right. I hit delete when I hit the wrong letter. Swore at the thing when it autocorrected.

> Beautiful: I don't even know your name.

I huffed, stared at my phone. I only knew hers

because of Jed and I still knew I was going to marry her. What was on her birth certificate wasn't going to make a difference because to me, she was Beautiful. However, when she found out I was South Wainright, her perspective of me might change. I wanted to solely be Hot Cowboy for as long as possible. To get her to fall for the guy, not the name. Not the bank account.

> Me: You said you felt it too. That was
>   from five minutes. No names. Just...
>   chemistry.
> Beautiful: Nothing good happens that
>   fast. I have to go. I have three places
>   to clean.

I groaned, ran a hand over the back of my neck. Typed out one word.

> Me: Tomorrow.
> Beautiful: Work tomorrow too. Always
>   work.

I paced the room, ready to climb in my truck and track her down, toss her over my shoulder and bring her back here. Tie her to my bed if I had to. Strip her bare and show her how it would be between us. Only pleasure. That it wasn't called love at first sight for nothing. One look and I knew. I stared at her last words. *Always work.*

That wasn't going to happen. I wanted her to work if it fulfilled her. I'd gone to art school even after listening to Macon bitch and complain, shout and demean me for wanting to be a pansy-ass artist ever since the third grade and I'd won a President's Day poster contest. I'd heard every one of the fucker's words, but never let his insults stick. I'd done what I wanted, become what I wanted.

If her dream was to clean other people's houses, then I'd support her. But if she was always working to make ends meet, that was different.

I had money I'd never touched. Enough where she wouldn't have to work if she didn't want to.

While I didn't like our exchange one fucking bit, at least she hadn't lied. She told me how she felt. I knew what the problem was. Obviously, she'd been hurt in the past. She'd rushed and it had gone to shit.

This wouldn't. This was different.

It had gone to shit because whoever that guy was wasn't the one for her. I was.

There was no other option for me but to be with her. It sure as fuck was fast. It didn't scare me though. It made me more determined than ever to prove her wrong. Nothing was going to hold me back now.

Some things *did* happen fast.

First, I had to get her in front of me. Get her here and then I'd show her. If words didn't do it, action would. I looked around my house. Grinned. I knew just the way.

5

MAISEY

THE ONE THING I liked about my cleaning job was the independence. While I had to follow the owner Nancy's strict cleaning methods that were expected by all of her employees, I wasn't stuck in a cubicle all day. I drove to the various houses I was assigned, did the work, then moved on to the next one.

The Wainright house was huge, but it was only three times a week. For so many rooms, not all were used. Most of them only needed to be dusted on occasion. North and her boyfriend, Jed, were the only two who lived in the house now, and they stuck mostly to the kitchen, great room and their bedroom.

Nancy said that there were only rare occasions when extra cleaning was needed before and after an event. The place was made for entertaining, but the last extra work at Billionaire Ranch—the name everyone called the place—was for Macon Wainright's wake in July.

Billionaire Ranch wasn't part of my route today, which was good since it ensured I didn't run into *him*.

I'd started by cleaning a hair salon before they opened at ten, then a house on the south side of town. The family had four kids, three dogs, a cat, and chickens so the place was chaotic and always took a little extra time. It was after lunch and I had a new home on my list, further out of town. As I drove and ate a bar that counted as my lunch, I checked the written instructions Nancy had given me, then put on my blinker as I turned down a dirt road. I patted the steering wheel, as if sorry for taking my aging car on bumpy roads. It didn't need any more rattles and loose parts.

When I lived in Billings and cleaned, we were sent out in pairs so no one was alone in a strange home. Safety in numbers. Out here, the town was so small, everyone knew everyone else. Or at least Nancy did.

She only took on clients she knew and trusted. She'd told me while some clients might bring in ample money, they weren't worth the headache. I certainly understood that and trusted her judgement. She paid on time and gave me cash.

I'd waitressed or worked for cleaning services since I was fourteen, even while I'd been going to college. While I wasn't thrilled about cleaning toilets, waitressing was harder. My back always ached after the end of a long shift, tips weren't guaranteed and not every customer was friendly. Cleaning was mostly done in an empty house, or the homeowner gave me plenty of room.

Except the hot cowboy yesterday. He'd come into the Wainright kitchen and sucked all the oxygen out of the place. And stole the thoughts from my head. I'd been mesmerized enough to hand over my cell and he shared his phone number.

The texts we'd shared this morning still had me questioning myself. I'd been mopping the tile floor at the beauty salon when my phone vibrated in my jeans pocket. I hadn't changed my mind overnight, but I'd wavered when he'd texted *Give US a chance.*

God, I wanted to. To call him, talk to him, date him, kiss him, fuck him, marry him.

He was right, there was something between us. Instant. Intense. Completely insane.

I laughed as I pulled up in front of an older farmhouse, turned off the car. Marry him? The guy had wanted to go out with me, not make babies. Maybe the cleaning supply fumes were getting to me. I lost all reason when it came to Hot Cowboy. I didn't even know his name and I was having insane thoughts about forever with him.

That was why I'd pushed him away. I was the only sane one in the Miles family. The levelheaded one. I thought before I fucked. That was probably why I never fucked. Or just the one time. I'd learned my lesson the hard way. On that and so many other things when it came to my mom, and especially Paisley.

I thought too much. I worried. I was jaded. Ruined by all the expensive lessons I'd learned.

But this guy was different. Paisley didn't know where I was. How I felt had nothing to do with her. She wasn't going to show up and lure him away. I had no competition from my identical twin.

Could I let my guard down though? The consequences were huge. I knew every one of them first-hand. I needed to let go. Go with my gut feelings for once. This guy? He made me crazy.

I was insane for even considering reciprocating his

interest. I felt like my mother who had zero self-control. Horrible judgement. Absolutely no self-preservation skills. No *look before you leap* mentality.

I wasn't going there. I couldn't. I'd learned too much by all the guys coming and going from our tiny trailer. And Paisley using men. Using me—in different ways—but without any kind of remorse.

I was paying for their actions. Literally. Sitting here and dwelling wasn't going to get the house clean, so I climbed out and grabbed my cleaning caddy from the backseat. The money earned from cleaning houses paid my small rent, fed me, and slowly built up my nest egg. I'd be able to get the mammogram and make one of my worries go away. The lump was just a hormonal cyst, not the C-word. The saved money wouldn't be going in a bank this time. I wasn't having her empty another account. It was one thing for her to steal my college money, another to delay the medical stuff. That was one negative behind looking exactly alike. At least for me. She'd benefited, that was for fucking sure.

Yeah, I wasn't bitter at all.

The fall air was crisp. Clouds had rolled in, and the temperature had dropped. It wasn't cold enough to snow, but there was frost on the ground in the mornings now. Snow would come soon and stick until spring.

The wind blew strong and I hurried up the porch steps. Setting my supplies down, I rang the doorbell. The place was two stories, wood siding. White paint. It was weathered, but not peeling. Maintained but there weren't any flowers. No rocking chair or swing. No welcoming doormat. I had to wonder if a bachelor lived here.

No one came to the door so I rang again.

Footsteps came from around the side of the house. Two men and one of them was definitely a bachelor. One I had been trying to avoid.

Hot Cowboy.

My heart raced and my cheeks heated as he and the other man stopped just off the porch.

A slow grin spread across Hot Cowboy's face. He hadn't shaved since I saw him and he'd grown some scruff. Of course it only accentuated the angle of his jaw and I wondered how it would feel against my thighs. Not that I'd ever had a guy's head there before, but I instantly imagined the position with him. My pussy clenched, eager for him. Why weren't my mind and body in sync?

"There's my beautiful girl," he murmured in that deep murmur.

Oh fuck. I was in trouble now.

"Banging the help. Nice," the other man said. I hadn't paid him much attention, but now I couldn't stop staring at him. Had he really said that? He was close to thirty with brown hair that was receding at a swift pace. While he wore jeans and a black, long-sleeved t-shirt advertising a motorcycle shop in South Dakota. He was unshaven, unkempt and there was no comparison between the two men on which one my ovaries liked.

Hot Cowboy wasn't thrilled with the guy's words. His hand shot out and gripped the guy's shirt. "What the fuck did you just say?"

The jerk's face went red, and he held his hands up in surrender. "Hey man, just stating the obvious."

"Leave my woman alone."

"You make your woman clean your house? I knew we'd get along."

"Cunningham, get the fuck off my property," Hot Cowboy snarled, then pushed him toward the parked pickup truck.

"So no commission then?" the guy called, climbing in the truck, laughing.

He peeled down the driveway, dust flying.

When all was quiet and we were sure he was gone,

Hot Cowboy came up onto the porch. I had to tilt my head back to meet his concerned eyes.

"Sorry about that," he said. "The fucker had no manners."

I'd met a jerky guy before. This one wasn't new.

"I... you want me to clean your house?" I almost squeaked. I wasn't confused, but I was flustered and that made the stupid question pop out. Of course he wanted me to clean his house. Nancy had given me the address.

"No fucking way do I want you to clean my house," he replied.

I blinked. "Oh... then..."

He saw the supply caddy, took it from me and set it on the porch. With a hand at the small of my back, he opened the door and ushered me into the house. "This is the only way I could think of to get in front of you again."

"You wanted to see me that much?"

We stood in the entryway. To the right was a family room, the left a dining room and directly in front of us stairs heading to the second floor. A hallway cut through the middle of the house which I assumed led to the kitchen at the back. The furniture was a mixture of older pieces, something a grandmother might have, and newer items, like a huge recliner by the stone fireplace.

He stepped back, crossed his arms over his chest and looked down at me. "Woman, what part of *give us a chance* was confusing?"

I swallowed. He wasn't mad, but he was frustrated. Which only added to my own frustration, so I crossed my arms to match his. "What part of *it would never work* is complicated?"

"How do you know it won't work? You said you felt it too... this connection." He pointed to me, then to himself. I sighed, took in his sturdy leather boots and worked my way up his body. He had on jeans and a plaid shirt, left untucked. The sleeves were rolled up showing off corded forearms, tanned from being in the sun and dusted with crisp brown hair.

I felt it all right. The intensity of his stare as it raked over me. I looked as I had the day before in my cleaning company t-shirt, jeans, and sneakers. My hair was pulled back in a ponytail, and I had no makeup on. Unlike his dark, masculine scent, I smelled like pine cleanser.

I turned away. Looking at him was too hard. The perfect guy who I was *very* attracted to was standing a few feet away. He wanted me. Enough to call Nancy and arrange for me to clean his house to get a chance to talk to me. It was oddly romantic, which made it even worse.

"Look, if you honestly aren't interested, fine," he said. "You can walk out that door and I'll never bother you again. I'm not a fucking stalker. At least be honest with me. Be honest with yourself."

I whirled back and had to push my glasses up. "I'm honest with myself." I waved my hand between us like he had. "I know what can happen. This, between us, is dangerous."

His brows went way up. "I went to school with Nancy's daughter. She wouldn't have sent you here if she didn't think you were safe. You think I'd hurt you?"

I quickly shook my head. "No. I know you wouldn't."

"How can you be so sure about that while saying it would never work?"

I looked up at the ceiling, then back at him. "Fine, it's not that it *won't* work. It *can't*."

"Why? Explain it to me." He closed the distance between us as if he finally couldn't help himself. Grabbing my upper arms in a gentle clench, he lowered his head and kissed me. It was as if he needed to get his lips on mine.

"Explain why this is bad because it feels so fucking

good to me," he whispered as his lips hovered over mine.

I didn't respond because it felt so fucking good to me, too. I pushed up onto my tiptoes and kissed him right back. Stupid, perhaps, but my mind wasn't in charge at the moment, even after my internal debate the whole drive out here. And... fuck me, his lips were gentle. Soft. Consuming. Then they weren't. He tipped his head and took it deeper. I whimpered because I felt it to my toes. His tongue found mine, tangled. Plundered. I melted and came alive. Sank and caught fire. Every crazy line of poetry that could describe a kiss, I felt.

When he lifted his head—I had no idea how long we'd kissed for—I was pressed against the nearest wall. When had we moved? His thigh was between my legs, and I was practically riding it. His hand was beneath my t-shirt and cupping my breast.

I licked my lips as I caught my breath.

"Walk out the door, beautiful," he dared, giving my nipple a little pinch through my bra. "Walk away from that."

He dropped his hand away and I missed it.

I couldn't go anywhere. I raised my fingers, touched my swollen lips. I'd been kissed before, but not like that. Not in a way that made me feel lost.

Overwhelmed. As if nothing else existed but the two of us. His hands and mouth on me. My nipple tingled, eager for his touch again.

I cleared my throat, tried to re-engage my mind, because I'd definitely lost it. One kiss and all reason fled, which was bad.

"My mother meets a guy and says she's in love," I said, trying to explain why I was resisting him, although not all that well. "It's instant. Amazing. He's *the one* she always says. He's going to take her out of the trailer park to his big house. Go on trips. Give her fancy clothes. A car. She quits her job and usually dyes her hair a different color blonde to look prettier. I think one guy got her some lingerie, but I was twelve and didn't ask and was glad the lace and silk distracted him from me and my sister."

His jaw clenched, but he stayed quiet.

"Instead of all the fancy promises, he moves into the trailer with us and within a few days, she's getting his beer while he watches football, his bare feet propped up on the coffee table. That was pretty typical of the losers."

I was sure he could hear my sarcasm and bitterness because while he didn't pull away, he moved his leg so I wasn't riding it any longer. He stroked my hair, and I shifted my gaze from the front of his shirt to his eyes. I saw heat there, but dark focus.

"Go on," he prodded, knowing there was more.

I licked my lips. Tasted him. "The guy sticks around for about two weeks. One made it two months." I shrug.

"Then what?"

"She gets dumped. Cries to me about men are all assholes and only want one thing."

He stepped back all the way, leaned against the opposite wall of the hallway. There was about three feet between us now. "You think I only want one thing from you?"

I shrugged again, my nipple tingling from that little pinch.

"With my mom, it all seems tawdry or cheap. This wasn't."

"No."

"But it made me lose my head," I admitted.

A slow smile crept across his face. "That's what it's supposed to do if it's done right. If you're with the right person."

I understood what he was saying. I *felt* the truth of it in how wet my panties were. Still...

"But it'll make me just like my mother," I whispered, looking away. "When I left, she was out of work, behind on the rent and trolling bars for a new guy."

"I hear what you're saying. You need control, especially over something that's happening really fast. Especially with something like this that's out of our control."

I blinked at him. Wow. He got it.

"It's out of control for me, too," he said. "This isn't one sided, beautiful. One look and I was done for."

God, he made me feel so good. Wanted. Cherished, even. I wasn't used to it, and it scared me. Was he saying all the right things to get in my pants? Would he fuck me and be done?

I'd kissed him back. I wanted him, too. This wasn't one sided. I had to decide if he was worth the risk because what if I was right? What if he'd be added to the long list of men who were assholes. Was he worth believing?

My mom had gobbled up all the lies every man had fed her. Over and over again. She never learned.

I'd seen through their bullshit when she hadn't. Right here, right now, this didn't feel the same.

It felt... more. That hope I felt, it grew to include him.

He took my hand. "Come on. I want to show you something."

I let him lead me down the hall and through his kitchen. I took in what I could as we went. The appliances were modern, but the house had a casual, homey feel. The place was neat. I didn't even see a dish in the sink.

He led me out the door and to a barn set back in a field, painted the same crisp white as the house.

Inside, the space was huge. One large room. While the house wasn't modern, the barn deceptively was and definitely not used for animals. There were skylights in the vaulted ceiling, the back wall a long row of sliding glass doors that let in even more light and offered a pretty view of the fields and the mountains in the distance.

Huge metal sculptures filled most of the space. Some were finished, some in various stages of work. Large and small sheets of metal leaned up against a wall. Buckets of scraps were lined up by a workbench. Fuel tanks were in a corner.

"What is all this?" I asked, wandering.

"My studio," he replied. "I'm a sculptor. I weld metal to make things."

I went over to one of the projects. It was a huge elk, life-size, made completely of different kinds of metal. Shiny sheets, corrugated sections. Nuts and bolts. Rusted rivets and other pieces that looked like they had come from a junkyard. Combined, it was stunning. While it was clunky and huge and heavy, the animal appeared to be moving, as if charging or bugling for a mate.

It had to weigh a thousand pounds. It was massive, manly. Aggressive. Bold. Just like the artist. This wasn't just *making things.*

He was really talented.

"You made this?"

He tucked his hands into his jeans pockets and nodded. He pointed toward the door. "That asshole was here because he was interested in a commission. He came into some money and wants something made."

Next to it was another animal piece, half done.

"You're... famous. They're amazing."

He replied to the praise with a chin lift. "I'm showing you these so you know I don't sit around and watch football. Well, every once in a while with my brother, but the only time you'll bring me a beer is if you're grabbing one for yourself and you're coming to sit in my lap."

"Oh."

He crooked his finger again, like he did the day before. I went to him.

"I want you," he said. Three words summed up how he felt.

"Just like that? You saw me, you want me, so you got Nancy to have me clean your house to get me here?"

"If you haven't figured it out yet, I'm a bossy guy. I didn't think tossing you over my shoulder at another job and kidnapping you was going to work."

I couldn't help but smile. "You're probably right."

"Give us a chance, beautiful. Fuck, I want more of those kisses." His gaze dropped to my body, raked over me as if he had X-ray vision. "On your mouth. Your body. I wondered yesterday if you were wet because I was hard as a fence post. I am now, too."

I glanced down and I couldn't miss the thick bulge in his jeans.

"But now I have to know," he continued. "Is your pussy all needy after that kiss?"

I gasped and squeezed my thighs together. He must have seen the subtle motion because he groaned and picked me up, carried me to a workbench and sat me on it. Nudging my knees apart, he stood between them. We were eye level.

His breath mingled with mine. I recognized his scent now. Craved it. His hands rested on my hips. Holding me. Waiting.

"Is it?" he prodded.

This was the moment where I had to decide. Tell the truth and he'd know I was into him just as much as he was into me, although he already knew. He wouldn't be pushing me if I wasn't into it. He wanted me to admit it. To consent to being right there with him.

"Yes," I whispered.

That one word and he groaned. His lips were back on mine. My hands went to his waist, slid around his back beneath his shirt. Felt the play of his muscles, the heat of his skin. My t-shirt lifted and we broke the kiss long enough for him to drop it onto the workbench beside me.

My ankles hooked about his hips as I tilted my head back. He kissed down my neck and across the swells of my breasts above my plain white bra. It felt so good, his lips. The rough calluses on his palms as he undid the clasp on my bra and cupped my bare breasts. He was the first to touch me like this because Tommy hadn't taken any time with me.

I cried out, suddenly frantic. Needy. My fingers went to his belt, and I tried to work the buckle open, but who could do such a task when a hot cowboy's mouth was latched onto my nipple?

He helped me, getting his jeans open and his dick

out in record time. Taking my hand from his back, he placed it on his hard length and wrapped my fingers around it. Barely. They couldn't even touch, he was that big. My pussy clenched in anticipation... and concern for it fitting. Tommy had taken my virginity in the back seat of his car and it had hurt. We'd skipped most of the steps and he'd only lifted my skirt and stuck it in me. I'd been dry and it had hurt so fucking bad, especially with a condom. He'd been a two-pump chump and that had been it.

I hadn't been eager like this, or wet. While I'd never seen Tommy's dick, it had felt big as he'd pushed it inside me. But nothing like this. I looked down.

It was huge. It was hot beneath my palm. The skin was taut and silky smooth, yet it was rock-hard. I'd never thought it was sexy to do this, but I'd never imagined myself being this aroused. I'd made him this hard.

Tommy had never made me feel like this. Wild, hot. Frantic. I'd been hotter for Hot Cowboy just looking at him across the Wainright kitchen than I had with Tommy. I'd been young and all I'd wanted was to lose my virginity. To get it over with. Hell, to get Tommy to want to be with me. Stupid, because it turned out, he'd been like all the other guys, into

Paisley more. Once she found out what he and I had done, she offered him more than spreading her legs in the back seat. She'd sucked Tommy's dick in the janitor's closet after US History class.

He'd dumped me for her talented mouth. Paisley had...

"Where'd you go, beautiful?" he asked, blowing on my nipple and watching it harden. His hand was still around mine on his dick showing me how he wanted me to move.

"I'm not good at this," I admitted, worried he'd think twice about this.

He looked up at me, those dark eyes meeting mine. A soft smile curved his lips. "You're doing just fine." I gave him a little squeeze and he muttered *fuck* under his breath.

I licked my lips. "I mean, I'm not very experienced."

His head popped up, eyes wide. "You're a virgin?" He looked me over as if he could tell.

Shaking my head. "No. Not officially, but I might as well be. You really don't want to know about my sex life, do you?"

His jaw clenched and he took my hand off his dick. "What you did before we met isn't my business. Unless the fucker hurt you. Then it is."

I thought of Tommy. I couldn't blame him for wanting Paisley instead of me. He'd been sixteen and horny. If I'd been able to suck chrome off a bumper back then—as he'd said Paisley could do—he'd have stuck around. I'd been stupid to think so much of him... of the *us* that hadn't actually existed.

"He didn't. It was one time."

He stroked my hair back. How he could be so gentle with his dick out, long, thick, and hard and pointing right at me, I had no idea. "You've only had sex once?"

I nodded, my cheeks turning pink. I was twenty and pretty much a virgin. What did he even think? I wasn't going to talk about Paisley. Explain why I didn't fool around with guys. Show any kind of interest in them. I wasn't going to *think* about her. Not while I was topless and with the hottest man I'd ever met.

"Fuck, woman. All the things I want to show you. Do you know how hot you are?"

I couldn't help but laugh. And blush. I wasn't used to compliments, especially when it came to my looks. Paisley might be my identical twin, but there was no comparison. "I'm not wearing sexy lingerie. I don't even own any."

He leaned down, kissed my nipple. "I'm a simple guy. I'll take naked over lace any day."

"You want an *us,* want me naked, but I still don't know your name."

He groaned and his eyes fell closed, rested his forehead against mine.

It was crazy to have come this far, to feel this much for a guy who I still only knew as Hot Cowboy.

He pulled back, looked at me. "South Wainright."

I stiffened.

South Wainright?

I flushed even hotter now. Oh shit. I was a fool. I felt like I was in some Disney movie falling for a prince in disguise.

I tried to shift away, his hands gripped my hips. "Hang on, beautiful. What's wrong?"

"You don't work at the Wainright Ranch."

He shook his head.

I blanched, panicked by what I might have said the day before. "Did I stick my foot in my mouth yesterday?"

He smiled. "No. You defended North. It was... admirable."

"South, you're rich," I said, sounding completely stupid. Of course he knew he was rich! God, if Paisley were here, she'd have already fucked him six ways to Sunday by now. He was the epitome of a sugar daddy. Hot and loaded. Her favorite.

"I am," he admitted, but didn't make a big deal of it. Maybe that was the difference between being loaded and broke.

My heart was hammering as if I'd run a marathon. I licked my lips. "I'm Maisey Miles."

He nodded. "Jed told me your name. Want to tell me why it sounds like you compare me being rich to being an axe murderer?"

"I didn't have my hand around your dick for your money." I wanted to make that very clear. Because my mom and Paisley—not that I wanted to think of either of them with their hands on a dick—equated money with pleasing a guy. Sure, he could open his wallet and probably hand me the cash I needed for the mammogram. No way would I ask him. I needed him to know I wanted him *only* for him. Nothing else.

"Your hand wouldn't be around my dick if I thought you did," he countered. "You wouldn't be here either. I don't invite women here." When I still seemed skeptical, he continued. "How many women do you think want me solely for my money?"

A lot. But I could think of one personally. Paisley. My mom, too, although South was too young for her. Although for billions, it wouldn't matter.

His eyes had heat in them, making them darker. Making them spark. He wasn't mad, but frustrated. I hadn't even considered he'd doubt relationships. Of course he had women falling all over him. South Wainright. He was literally the biggest bachelor catch ever. Besides his two younger brothers. Gorgeous, rich. And he had a huge dick, and I was positive he knew how to use it.

"I don't want your money. I didn't even know who you were." I had to make it very clear to him about that. A mammogram was different than a trip to Mexico or shiny jewelry, but it didn't matter. I wouldn't be *want, want, want.* The second I asked him for money turned me into my mother. As if all I could offer was my body in exchange.

He nodded and he sighed. "I know. I think you wish I wasn't a Wainright."

I bit my lip. "Money... it's complicated."

The corner of his mouth kicked up. "No fucking kidding. I had to trick you into coming here. That's not what I'm used to."

I bet not.

"Tracy Dennis. High school. She expected me to get her a fancy dress for prom. Maria Dominguez. Freshman year of college. She looked me up online. Tried to trap me by drugging me and said we slept together. That I got her pregnant."

I gasped, having never considered a guy being roofied.

"Getting tested for every STD wasn't fun before she finally fessed up that we never slept together." He paused, ran a finger down my cheek. "Alana Bronson. Wanted an internship at Wainright Holdings."

I held up my hand. "Got it. You can't tell if a woman wants you or your money."

No way would I ask him for a dime. Ever.

He set his hands on the workbench on either side of me, leaned in.

"Exactly. Beautiful, you think I'd rush into something with only knowing a woman's first name if I didn't know for a fucking fact it was real?" he asked. "Besides, it's not rushing if it's fucking right. Why waste time?"

While I'd been worried he wanted me for all the wrong reasons, he'd trusted his gut and wanted me, and only me, for the right ones. And after all the women who'd used him.

I couldn't see anything but him. His gaze was open. Eager. Needy. Potent. That dark stare was mesmerizing. It said everything. It didn't waver. It didn't doubt. He wanted me and I was pushing him away because of my mother and sister? If I walked away, wouldn't they win? I was wary, but should I be stupid?

"I won't hurt you. I'd never want to hurt you. After the shit I've been through, my heart's on the line, too."

Why waste time? The answer was instant and came from *my* heart.

No.

I melted. Gave up the fight. Let all the anxiety, the tenseness go. My breasts were uncovered, the cooler air making my nipples hard. His dick was out. We weren't completely bare, but we'd shared of ourselves. Deeply.

Somehow, I trusted South. Trusted him more than I had anyone before. I wanted him. So I wrapped my hand around his dick again, stroked him from root to tip as my eyes met his. "No. You're right. Why waste time? This is real. I want you. I want *us.*"

6

HOLY FUCK. I had the girl of my dreams stroking my dick. I wasn't taking her for the first time on my work-bench, but I didn't have much blood left in my brain to process. I gripped her hand, stilled her movement. "Beautiful... fuck, just... shit."

I scooped her up with a hand cupping her ass and carried her over to the leather couch in the corner. Sometimes I got deep into my commissions, losing track of time, of whether I ate or slept. A few years ago, I'd dragged it out of the house for the few occasions I was too done in to make it to my bed. I was thankful for it now, lowering Maisey onto it and settling over her. There was no way I could wait to kiss and touch her long enough to leave the studio.

Somehow, she hadn't let go and kept right on stroking me.

I stilled her, gripping her hand once again.

She looked up at me, eyes wide. "Am I doing it wrong?"

Fuck, I was twenty-nine years old and a woman was asking me that. I hadn't heard that question since high school. Maisey was so much younger and *very* inexperienced. While I didn't want to think of any guy getting his hands on her—or his dick in her—I was thankful I didn't have to worry about it being her first time. Of it hurting. Still, her sweetness was endearing. My dick pulsed in her palm thinking about how I was going to get her all dirty.

"Just right." My dick wasn't happy, but I removed her hand. "If you keep it up, this'll be over too soon."

"Oh."

I kissed her then, long and hard. When she was reassured, I worked on getting off the rest of her clothes. It wasn't hard, flinging sneakers and jeans, panties and socks over my shoulder. I was never going to look at this couch in the same way again because she was gorgeous. Bare and beautiful. I hadn't done figure drawings since college—not my thing—but I itched to pull out the charcoals and put this moment down on paper.

Not giving her a second to become shy or embarrassed, I kissed down her body, taking time to suck on each of her nipples until she was writhing and tugging on my hair, then lower to lick around her navel. Then lower still.

"South," she said, her fingers tugging.

I glanced up at her from my spot between her thighs. "Ever done this before?"

She shook her head. Her ragged breathing made her tits sway.

Fuck. Pre-cum dripped from the slit. I swiped it away with my thumb.

I settled onto my knees on the floor, raised a foot onto the back of the couch so she was nice and wide. Fuck, she was so pretty. Pink. Swollen. Wet.

"I don't wax," she said, her face averted. "I mean, I shave and all, but my sister told me guys don't like to dig for clams."

I couldn't help but laugh. "Fuck, beautiful. Your pussy's perfect."

I didn't wait a second longer. I sucked on her inner thigh, left a little red mark, then shifted to taste her. Hell, I had to get her to come on my mouth. It was my mission in life to pleasure her. Her back arched and she cried out when I licked up her slit. I took my time, watching her, learning what she liked. She was sweet and musky. And responsive. Her clit was a hard little pearl and I flicked it with the tip of my tongue.

That set her off. I added a finger, circling her entrance, then curling it inside. That finished her off.

Her inner walls clenched around me. Her thighs squeezed against my ears. Her fingers tugged at my hair.

Fuck, yes.

Writhing and moaning. Lost. Wild. Passionate. She'd come in less than a minute, set off like a firecracker. When she slumped against the couch, wilted and catching her breath, I kissed her inner thigh, sucked on that same spot again. She lowered the raised leg.

"You... your turn. Now." She curled her fingers in a beckoning motion.

I grinned, wiped my mouth with the back of my hand. "Yes, ma'am."

I pulled my wallet from my back pocket, grabbed the condom stored within and tossed it onto the sofa. I stood, shucked my clothes.

"Oh my God," she whispered once I was bare and my dick pointed straight at her.

"It'll fit, beautiful."

She rolled her eyes, but that smile. I had a feeling it was only for me. The way she looked right now. Relaxed. Comfortable with me.

Trusting.

Grabbing the condom, I tore off the wrapper and rolled it on.

"You still good?" I asked. I didn't want to stop. My dick was going to fall off if it didn't get some relief, but I'd sooner have it do just that than to hurt her.

"Yes."

While she wasn't a virgin, if she'd only had sex once, it might be uncomfortable, at least to start.

I dropped onto the leather—bare assed and I didn't give a shit—and said, "Climb on. Take me for a ride."

She eyed me, then my dick. Pushing herself up, she crawled onto my lap, my dick pressed between us.

"You still wet and ready for me?"

She nodded.

I set my hands on her bare hips, her body so lush and soft.

"Up on your knees. That's it." I held the base of my dick as she adjusted, lowering and getting the crown right at her entrance. Her small hand settled on my shoulder. Her tits. Fuck, they were right there.

But I felt the heat of her pussy through the condom, and I gritted my teeth.

"Take your time, lower yourself down. Fuck," I said on a long exhale.

She was tight. Really fucking tight. Hot. Thankfully dripping wet because she slid right onto me, gravity helping her along.

Her eyes widened and she bit her lip as she twisted and circled, raised and lowered in little pumps until she sat right on my lap.

"Oh my God," she whispered, eyes closed.

I was panting now, trying with all my might not to grab her hips and thrust up into her. Hard.

When she lifted her lashes, her gaze met mine. "There's my beautiful girl," I murmured, then tapped her glasses at the bridge of her nose. "You need these?"

Instead of answering, she took them off and set them on the arm of the couch.

"You ready to move? Please say you're ready to move."

Her laugh was soft and melodic and her inner walls clenched.

My fingers squeezed.

She lifted up, then dropped down. Eyes widening. She did it again with a circle of her hips.

"That's it." Fuck, it felt so good. The barn could catch fire around us and I wouldn't even know.

She caught on quickly, giving over to what felt right for her. She didn't hold back. Her fingers gripped my shoulders. Her head fell back. She gasped. Writhed.

I licked my thumb and slid it between us, circled her hard clit.

Her eyes flared and met mine.

"Us," I murmured. I'd never felt closer to anyone in my life. I didn't remember my mother. Only hints of her remained. A scent. A laugh. Macon, I wanted to forget. Being his son, I wanted to burn from my mind. My siblings, well, we were just reconnecting now. I'd never told a woman I loved her. I'd never found sex to be more than a release. But this, right here, right now... it was what it was supposed to be like.

All consuming.

Like being home.

"Come for me," I breathed.

She did after fucking herself on me a few times. Her tits bobbed and when she came, she clenched down around me as she gasped.

I gritted my teeth. Watched. She was so fucking beautiful.

Once her inner walls stilled, I spun us around so

she was the one sitting on the couch. Then I tugged her down so she was slumped, her hips just off the edge. Dropping to my knees, I remained inside her, but lined up perfectly to fuck her hard.

I was too far gone to go slow. She'd used me as she needed to find her pleasure. I was going to use her to find mine. But the way she was looking at me, the way she lifted her hips into my every thrust, she was right there with me.

Our bodies slapped together. Sweat dripped down my temples. Our breathing grew louder. My balls drew up and I couldn't hold back, slamming deep and emptying into her.

Maisey shifted her hips, still needing more. I pulled out as I held the base of the condom, then flipped her onto her stomach. She was bent over the couch, her ass up. Her pussy was red from the hard fucking and I fingered her, slipping one digit inside, then two. Curling them, I found her g-spot and rubbed as my thumb found her clit.

"South," she murmured.

I gave her a playful swat. "Suck a greedy pussy."

Her inner walls clenched, and she came again as I wrung the last bits of pleasure from her. I took care of the condom, tied it up and tossed it into a nearby trash can.

Scooping her up, I settled onto the couch with her tucked into my side. I grabbed the blanket off the back, dropped it on us, tucked her head onto my chest and stroked her sleek hair. I was sweaty and it was warm, but this was perfect. Cozy.

Kissing the top of her head, I closed my eyes. Settled into the feeling of being in the perfect place with the perfect person.

7

M AISEY

"STAY."

I looked over my shoulder as I slid my bra straps up, hooked it at the back. South, sprawled out on the couch, naked, was a mouthwatering sight. My pussy ached and I couldn't help the smile that spread across my face. I was relaxed. Happy.

That was what sex was supposed to be. A religious experience. Filthy dirty. And with a guy with zero inhibitions and willing to do any kinky thing I wanted? *Ahmazing.*

He was so worth it.

I shook my head. "I've got two more houses to clean."

"I'll call Nancy and tell her I'm a needy client who needs extra attention."

I gently smacked his rock-hard abs. He took the opportunity to tug me on top of him and kiss my lips. His skin was warm and I breathed in his scent.

God, he was incredible.

"You will do no such thing!" I laughed and he smiled. All those rough edges South seemed to have were softened now. It felt like I was seeing a side of him he didn't share with others. Him, like this, was a secret, something intimate between us. He'd put himself out there for me. Even now. Naked and not wanting me to go.

He was so tempting... I wasn't even thinking of his body. I liked the man, too. I wanted to stay and talk to him. Learn everything about him. And have more sex.

"I can't get fired," I told him. "I need the work and Nancy's been really nice to me. I don't want to let her down."

"You're not from around here." He didn't state it as a question.

I shook my head. "Billings. I moved here in July."

He brushed my hair back. I had no idea where my hair tie went. Good thing I had extras in my car. "Why here? You dream of small-town life or something?"

I couldn't help but roll my eyes.

Something had definitely changed between us. We had a connection that I'd never felt with anyone else but talking about my life wasn't easy. It felt good to keep that separate. Like putting my past in a box high on a shelf where it could collect dust and be forgotten.

Still, I had to share, even a little bit.

"I told you about my mom." He offered a slight nod. He raised an arm, tucked his hand behind his head and gave me his full attention. I looked down at the smattering of hair on his chest and idly played with it. "My sister's just like her. They're... selfish. You're a guy, but you know how sisters share clothes and all that? Well, mine thinks that goes for boyfriends and money."

He frowned. "She stole from you?"

I nodded. I wasn't going to tell him she'd emptied my bank account. Took what I'd saved to pay for my next semester of college.

"Yeah. I had to get out of there. I know North's your sister." If he noticed I was turning the conversation back to him, he didn't let on.

"Yeah. I have younger brothers, East and West."

"I'm sure everyone asks you about your names."

He twirled my hair around his finger and tugged me down. We kissed, slow and easy, then he answered.

"My mother's maiden name was Southforth. That's the name I got. She died when I was four."

"I'm sorry," I murmured, kissing his chin.

He shrugged.

"You lost your dad recently, too." I'd started cleaning at the ranch after the man's death, but I'd learned some details about the family from Nancy and the others I worked with.

He stiffened beneath me, then carefully sat up, moving me so I was at the end of the couch. Grabbing his jeans, he stood and put them on, but didn't touch the zipper. This was a casual intimacy I never knew existed.

I felt the shift in him, like a curtain was drawn over his emotions. All the warm and fuzzies we shared were gone. "What?" I asked, suddenly confused. "What did I say?"

He turned to me, squatted down in front of me so we were eye to eye. His workspace was behind him, but I didn't see any of it. Only him. "You're perfect, beautiful. You can't do anything wrong."

I pursed my lips, but I loved his sweet words. "I said something."

He tucked my hair back again, as if he couldn't stop touching it, but his shoulders were tense. I studied his eyes, and they were a little haunted. "I can tell it's hard for you to talk about your mom. Your sister. We have a lot in common with our families. Trust issues. Lying. Macon Wainright died in July. Turns out, Macon actually is my dad, but not the others', which is different than what the town thinks. We're still trying to figure it all out. What it means. He was an asshole and I have his blood in my veins."

I could tell it was worse than that, but I didn't push. "You're not an asshole to me."

He gave me a small smile. "When will I see you again?" he asked.

I sighed, thinking about the rest of my day. "When I finish working, I'm going home to crash. Someone wore me out," I added the last in a playful tone.

I got the response I wanted as he gave me one of his smiles.

"I'll come to you." He closed his eyes. "Shit. I forgot. I'm meeting West tonight. Guy's night. I can't get out of it or he'll never shut up."

"It's fine." Except a little part of me thought it wasn't. That I was already spoiled to having him around. It definitely was the orgasms. "I'll be asleep by nine anyway. Tomorrow, I'm back Wainright Ranch. God, your ranch, right?"

"The whole spread belongs to me and my sister and brothers. Technically, the house, too. But it's really North's. Where she and Jed will raise their family someday. This farmhouse is mine. It's enough."

"I'll be there tomorrow starting at eight," I told him.

"Then I'll come there. Distract you. Carry you into one of the empty rooms and do dirty things." He winked. "Just the thing I need."

I laughed, although secretly I wanted him to do just that. "I'm not losing my job."

"I have an in with your boss."

I shook my head. "No way. No one will say anything about you, but I'll be the woman who slept with the boss's brother. Or I'm after you for your money."

His smile slipped. "Shit, that's a fucking double standard. Fine. No carrying."

I stood and South did too. Grabbing my clothes, I got dressed.

"I have to go," I said, wistfully. "I'm behind already."

He stroked my hair. "One more kiss, beautiful, and I'll let you go."

As I sank into it, I knew I didn't really want him to. This was so perfect. Too good to be true. Because no matter what he said, nothing good lasted. But what we had? I was sure going to try.

8

SOUTH

"WHAT THE FUCK'S up with you?" West asked, slowly working the label off his beer bottle.

He sat across from me in a booth at the bar on Main Street, the only one in our small town. Had I known it was line dancing night, I'd have suggested meeting somewhere else. I didn't dance, but the two other guys in our group did. Or, they did when there were cute women to do it with.

"What the hell are you talking about?" I asked. I kicked back, stretched one of my legs outside the booth.

"You hate this shit," he replied. "You only come out with us because listening to me bitch at you the rest of the month is worse than showing up."

"Whatever," I countered.

"I thought you had a new client today."

I sat forward, took a swig of my beer, then leaned back. Restless. I'd told West about Micah Cunningham calling me and interested in me sculpting something for him. It wasn't anything new. I got calls all the time. I didn't have an agent and handled my own business. "I did but turns out he's a fucking asshole. This town's got less than ten thousand people. You'd think the chances of dealing with shitty people would be so much less. Anyway, not happening." I made my own decisions on what commissions to take, and it wasn't going to be with Cunningham. No one insulted a woman like that. No one insulted *my* woman.

"Are you pissed about that or the DNA results?"

I gave him a look. "I take the work I want. Like I'd let some fucker get to me."

He tipped his head down, eyed me closely. "Isn't that what Macon's doing?"

I glared at him. I wasn't going to tell him he was right. Instead, I told him off. "Fuck you. You don't have his blood."

He rolled his eyes. "Whatever. You make it out to be poison or something. He's dead. Now what the fuck's really up with you?" he repeated.

I frowned. The fucker from earlier I could shrug off. Macon, I'd have to deal with. Somehow. But it was Maisey that was under my skin. "I'm not in the mood to be here," I mumbled. I could be in her bed, holding her while she slept. Instead, I was in the overly loud, overly crowded bar with a meddling brother and two guys on the prowl.

He leaned forward, set his forearms on the table. "Yeah, that's fucking obvious."

West was a year younger than me. Taller. Heavier, which made him a shit brickhouse. He was a rancher through and through. Liked the wide-open spaces and big skies. He'd gone off to college, like North had secretly bargained with Macon for, but he'd come back for the land. Skipping the big house or any of the Wainright property to run, he'd bought a ranch of his own. Raising cattle and horses was his job and he loved it. It made him the most easygoing of the four of us, with North being a busy CEO and East a university professor in Bozeman. While I kept my head behind a welder's mask most of the time and in my studio, West spent his days outdoors. He was patient as fuck. He was also a hell of a lot more social than me, probably because he needed human contact after talking to cows and horses all day. He'd pulled me into these once-a-month guys' nights. The one time I cancelled, he'd done just as he'd said, annoyed the shit out of me for missing it.

A waitress set down four more beers and he thanked her with a big smile and a wink before she moved on.

"That. There." He pointed in the direction of the disappearing waitress.

"What?"

"You didn't even look at her."

I frowned. "Who? The waitress? Isn't that Lia Nelson, Trace's sister?"

"Yeah. All grown up now. She was *looking* at you. Leaned in, flashed her tits."

I widened my eyes. "Lia? She flashed her tits?"

He sat back, sighed. He let go of his beer bottle and ran a hand over his face. "Fine, she flashed some cleavage, but you wouldn't have even known if she had *Fuck me* tattooed across her forehead."

I shrugged. "I'm not interested in Lia or tits flashed in my face at a bar."

Except I thought of one set of perfect tits that had been in my face earlier.

He pointed at me. "Exactly. Why is that?"

"Why am I not interested in a waitress? Do I usually give them my number?"

He didn't say anything, just stared at me and waited.

The song changed and there were a few whoops as people lined up for another familiar dance.

"Fine. I met someone," I admitted. He was going to keep at it until I told him about Maisey. She was the reason why I didn't pay attention to the waitress, or any other woman in the bar. My eyes—and my dick—were content on one specific woman. Unfortunately, she was home in her bed. Without me.

He grinned. "I knew it. Kylie at the coffee shop?"

I frowned as I thought of who he was talking about. "The one with the braid? She's... what? Nineteen?"

Shit. Maisey couldn't be much older. For some reason, age was an issue thinking about Kylie, who was West's neighbor's youngest daughter, but not Maisey. I liked her sweet and innocent. Not so much anymore after what we'd done in my studio.

"Fine, not her," he said. "Who?"

I smiled, thinking of my beautiful girl. Of her smile. Of what she looked like when I filled her full. How she sounded when she came with a guy for the first time. Not any guy.

Me.

Fuck, I was hard. I shifted in the booth.

"Maisey Miles. She cleans the big house," I explained.

His brows winged up. "You bagged the maid?"

I clenched my jaw, leaned forward. "She's not a fucking maid. She's a professional house cleaner. She works. Makes money. Just so happens the big house is one of her places. Don't fucking put down anyone who's trying to earn a living," I snapped.

He held his hands up as if afraid I'd punch him from across the table.

"It's like that?" he asked after studying me some more.

I nodded. "Yeah, it's like that."

He slowly shook his head. "North found Jed. Now you. Tell me about her."

He wasn't prodding now, only curious. We'd never done these kinds of male bonding, brotherly chats before. We'd had women and we'd talked about them some, but this was different. Those who came before were quick, fun fucks, but I'd never gotten to know them. Not like I wanted with Maisey.

"She's new to town," I told him. "She's steering clear of some shit with her family."

He laughed. "Who isn't?" he asked, then took a

pull on his beer. The song ended and another one started right up.

"What else?" West asked.

I thought of Maisey. "Dark hair. Five-two. Glasses. Shy. Defended North when she thought I was talking shit about her."

"When can we meet her?"

"Find your own woman," I countered, not interested in any guy laying eyes on my woman. Even West.

The bar was crowded and a little rowdy. I hadn't seen Matty or Duggar in a while, the other two guys in our group, but that wasn't new. We were here together for guys' night, but they were spending more time picking up women than hanging with us.

Shouts and clapping drew West's attention. He whistled and a slow smile spread across his face. "I think I might have done just that."

Curious as to who had drawn his attention, I turned and looked over the top of the booth. By the bar, a woman was standing between two men and they were squeezing lime slices over her bare shoulders, the juice sliding down her exposed skin and to her cleavage. In her red dress with thin straps, there was a lot of bare skin. Next, they licked salt off their hands—which they must have already put there before I'd started watching—then downed a shot. Most likely tequila. Leaning in at the same time, they licked the dribbles of lime juice off her, stopping at her tits. Her hands cupped the back of their heads and held them to her chest.

I stood, not to get a better view, but because I was fucking pissed. It wasn't just any woman the men were pretty much nipple sucking, but Maisey.

My Maisey. The one who was supposed to have gone home and crashed after work. It was after nine and she definitely wasn't in bed.

Her dark hair was artfully tousled, long down her back. It looked just fucked. I knew that first-hand. Her glasses were gone, and her makeup enhanced how pretty she was. The dress accentuated how fucking hot and curvy her body was. To everyone in the bar.

The guys finally lifted their heads, and they were grinning. Eager to fuck. They high fived each other and Maisey put her finger on one guy's lower lip. He bit it and she giggled. I couldn't hear the sound, but the action made her tits jiggle, which the other guy watched, practically drooling.

West came to stand beside me, took a pull on his beer. "That's pretty hot."

Maisey had been fucking with me. No, she'd fucked me, then moved on. It looked like she was going to get lucky with two guys tonight. And that didn't include me.

I'd wondered if I'd been too rough with her, if she was sore after how hard I took her, but now I had to wonder if I'd been too gentle. Too nice. Too... whatever. That she hadn't gotten what she'd wanted from me and needed to get her freak on with these two cowboys.

I didn't blame the guys, even though I wanted to punch their teeth in. Maisey was giving both of them the green light.

I had to wonder how many guys she worked over. If her needs were that insatiable. Fuck, I needed to get tested again. We'd used a condom, but if she was this horny, this much of a player, I wanted to be sure my dick wasn't going to fall off.

"Why do you look like you want to kill a whole bunch of people?" West asked, nudging my arm.

"That woman."

Out of the corner of my eye, I saw his grin. "You want her? I'll play wingman, but those two hanging off her might not be too happy."

"Want her? I *had* her."

He turned his head, stared at me.

I was so fucking pissed. Even after telling her about Macon, about the women who'd used me, she'd been faking it. No, there was no way she'd faked that orgasm. The way her pussy had rippled and clenched my dick. That had been real. But how many other guys was she getting orgasms from these days?

"You fucked her?" West asked, then paused. He must have seen the way I was grinding down my back molars. "Oh. Oh, shit. That's Maisey?"

I nodded once.

"She doesn't look shy to me."

I glared at him.

"Confront her. Find out what her deal is," he advised.

"I'm not a fucking girl out to stir up drama. While I thought she was all in, we barely know each other," I admitted, saying the truth out loud. "I didn't give her a ring. Didn't promise her anything."

Only pretty much fucking bared my soul. I'd thought the connection we had, when my dick had been buried deep inside her, had been more than just a quick fuck.

"Shit, I'm so fucking stupid."

"Not the first guy to go stupid for a body like that."

I turned to West. Growled. "She *lied* to me. She could've just said she wanted a no strings fuck."

"You'd have been okay with that?" he asked, studying me.

I gnashed my teeth together, remembering how it had felt with her. That while I'd thought it was something special, she'd probably had her mind on her next catch. Or two.

"No. Watching those guys all over her makes me want to... fuck." I ran my hand over my hair. "She lied. That's all I can think of right now."

"What's the saying? Some author came up with it. Love's like a fart. If you have to force it, it's probably shit."

I stared at him. "What the fuck are you talking about?"

He held up his hands, nodded. "Nothing. Nevermind. I get it."

Yeah, he probably did. After Macon, it was hard to trust or believe the shit anyone said. I'd let Maisey in, all the way.

I'd gotten off, but if all it had been was a lie, then all I really got for it was watching excessive PDA of her with two men.

"I'm outta here," I said, resigned to feeling like shit. I'd gone with my gut, my instant feeling of attraction. Hell, it had been more than that. Maybe it had been indigestion or bowel problems instead because I'd been so fucking wrong. Learning the truth about Macon and now this? Yeah, the only action my dick was going to see for a long time was with my hand. "I got commissions lined up. Maisey got what she wanted earlier. I guess so did I. She moved on. I am too."

"Sure you are," he replied, slapping me on the shoulder.

I turned toward the exit, thankful for the crowded dance floor. No way was I letting her see me. To know she'd pissed me off. That while she was all woman, she was acting like the guy in the relationship. Fuck him and forget him, then move on.

There was nothing wrong with that, if everyone was on board.

I had been, but for something else.

She was like a car wreck. Even as I neared the door, I had to watch her. One of the guys tugged her by the hand toward the bathrooms. The second man followed. What was going to happen next was obvious, especially since her hand was cupping his crotch as they walked.

Fuck.

I turned away, went out into the parking lot. West was behind me.

"You going to be okay?" he asked.

I spun and faced him, set my hands on my hips. Stared down at my boots in the dark. "You saw her.

She's hot as fuck. I tapped that and emptied my balls. Just remind me next time to go for Lia and the tit flashing."

"You lie for shit," he replied, studying me, although it was late and only a few exterior lights lit our faces. "You're going to shut yourself in that barn again?"

I strode toward my truck, leaving him behind. "Looks that way."

I'd go to the studio and get lost in my latest sculpture. I had a section ready to weld. I wanted to get lost in a bottle of whiskey but the one thing I didn't do was drink and work since the welding arcs got to about ten thousand degrees. I'd burn the shit out of myself, or burn the place down. Or get killed while doing both by blowing up the barn.

Except when I went back to my studio, all I was going to see was that couch where we'd fucked. That wasn't going to work. Whiskey it would be. The sculpture could wait. "Coming with me?" I called over my shoulder. "Or are you going to watch Matty and Duggar hook up?"

He jogged and caught up with me. Clearly, he was worried. "So much for guys' night. What do you have in mind?"

I thought of the couch. "A bonfire."

$\mathcal{M}$ AISEY

HE DIDN'T SHOW. While the Wainright house was enormous and it was easy to miss hearing people coming and going, I'd listened for South instead of my music through my earbuds. I also was overly diligent in window scrubbing, keeping a watch for his truck. And him. I hadn't missed North's return in the helicopter or when Jed showed up with their two dogs trailing his heels. I couldn't ask either of them after South.

Hey, I had sex with your brother and it was incredible. He said he was going to meet me here and carry me into one of your quieter rooms and go at it again. Have you heard from him because my panties are ruined since my pussy's craving his big dick?

North was nice, but not *that* nice.

As the morning wore on, I was nervous and antsy. I might feel desperate to see him, but I knew smothering a guy wasn't the way to go. I'd learned that advice from Mom. Maybe he got into his sculpture and lost track of time.

When my tasks were complete, I wanted to linger, thinking something might have held him up, but I had another house to clean. The rest of the day, I checked my cell incessantly, ensuring the ringer hadn't been turned off or that the battery hadn't died. He didn't call or text.

By the time I returned to my little house, I wondered if he'd been in an accident. Maybe he was hurt and in the hospital. But then, North would have known and neither she nor Jed had looked upset. Maybe it had happened after I left. Maybe... maybe I really was turning into my mother.

While I'd gone to bed around nine as I'd told him, I'd barely slept, tossing and turning once again, this time thinking of what we'd done together. How my body had come alive beneath his touch. I still ached in places.

He was literally impossible to forget.

It seemed that I was.

I paced and stared at my phone, wondering if I should call him. My finger hovered over Hot Cowboy in my contacts. I hadn't wanted to change it because to me, he was all that and more. After my shower, I gave in, but the call went right to voicemail. I didn't leave a message. I remembered all of the times my mom paced the trailer, calling and calling the men who'd fucked her and left her. The messages she'd left, getting more desperate with each one.

No. I wouldn't call again. I couldn't. If he didn't want me, then so be it. I refused to turn into exactly what I hated.

The next day, I had no choice but to go to work instead of staying in bed with the blankets over my head. He hadn't called. Hadn't texted.

By the time I got home at the end of the day, I knew. He wasn't going to get in touch with me. He'd gotten what he wanted, just like every guy who'd offered my mom sweet and promising words. I slid down the door and sat, knees bent, and cried. For believing South. For falling for his shit, even after all the second-hand experience I had. For hoping. For him destroying that hope, just as I'd worried he would.

I was the biggest loser ever. Why hadn't I learned?

Worse, why did I care so much? It had only been sex. Good sex. Soul baring, I'd thought. For both of us.

Yet, he'd ghosted me. If it had just been a one-off, why had he said all those things? Why had he been *all in* if he'd only planned to fuck me? Why not just say he wanted to have a good time. Give me a few orgasms, but no strings.

Why did he lead me to think he was into me? With shaky fingers, I scrolled through my texts. *Give US a chance,* he'd written.

"Why would he say that?" I said aloud, tears starting to stream down my cheeks.

Because he knew just how to get in my pants. I wasn't an easy lay—or so I thought—and he knew just the right way to play me. He'd lied.

The knock on the door startled me. It was him! God, I'd been wrong. He'd been caught in a ditch and just climbed out. Whatever the reason, it didn't matter. He was here.

My heart thumped so loudly I was sure he could hear it. I wiped at my face, sniffled. I wasn't a pretty crier, but I had to hope it wasn't that bad.

I flung open the door, but it wasn't South.

"Hey, sissy."

It was Paisley.

She pushed past me into my house, taking it all in.

I had my hand on the door as I stared at her. Stunned.

My stomach dropped and a mixture of anger and misery set in. She'd found me. My peace and quiet was over.

"Nice place."

She didn't mean it. The house was fine. Basic. Simple. Cheap. Yet it was safe and clean and all mine. It had been until a few seconds ago.

There wasn't much for her to look at, so she did her full circle then faced me.

Since we were identical, we obviously looked the same. Except as twins aged, one could gain extra weight, change her hair color. Style it differently. Get tattoos. Often there were obvious ways to tell who was who. But not with me and Paisley. Her hair was just like mine. Brown. Long. Simply styled. No obvious tattoos or scars. She hadn't gained weight. Or muscle. In short, it was her goal to look exactly like me because she couldn't use it—me—to her advantage otherwise.

The only outward difference was that she wore contacts and I didn't.

"What are you doing here?" I asked.

She cocked her head in a way I was very familiar with since I did it too.

"I wanted to say thanks for the trip."

I stayed by the door, left it open. She wasn't staying because her words were like battery acid on my skin.

"You want me to say you're welcome for taking all my money and going to Mexico? I don't need to go down the list of things you did to me, do I? Like identity theft, maybe?"

"Identity theft is a stretch since we look exactly the same," she countered, sniffing and studying her fingernails.

"We might look alike, but that's it." I sighed. "I had to drop out of school."

"Oh, please. You were always with your nose in a book. Live a little."

"How can I when you take all my money?" I countered. "I was less than a year from getting my nursing degree. It would have been a solid job, a career."

I wasn't the bad guy here, but narcissists twisted things around so the blame fell squarely on someone else.

She was mad at me for her taking my money.

"I have nothing for you, Paisley. You stole it all. My car's not worth anything." It hadn't been when I'd bought it at a used car lot. Now, it was on its last legs and had to keep praying to the car gods that it would last a little longer. I couldn't work if I didn't have transportation and I had a feeling repairing it would cost more than replacing it.

"Why can't I come visit my sister?" She turned and plopped down on my ratty couch, crossed her legs.

I stared up at the popcorn textured ceiling. "What part of you stole all my money is confusing? I clean houses and make a little over minimum wage. I don't even have a bank account." Or cash for a fucking mammogram to make sure I wasn't dying.

She leaned forward. "A little birdy told me you work at Billionaire Ranch."

I frowned, suddenly even more wary. "How do you know about that place?"

She shrugged. She wore a red sweater a little too bright for my tastes.

"A little birdy."

"You mean a guy with a big dick."

She smiled slyly.

Yeah, I was right. She hadn't just showed up in town and swung by. She'd been scoping me. Seeing what I was up to. Seeing how she could use me again.

"Two guys, actually."

Two? Not a surprise at all. Where I'd pretty much lost my virginity with South the day before, Paisley had given it up back in seventh grade. No doubt she was game for something a little wilder by now.

"Lovely," I replied sarcastically.

"You clean at Billionaire Ranch. I drove by. The place is huge. I'm sure you can find something to share with your sister."

She wanted me to steal from the Wainrights? I'd be the one getting caught. I'd be the one who'd lose her job. Besides the fact that working for Nancy was all that kept me from being homeless, South would see it as getting even. I was upset he'd ghosted me, but I wasn't going to get revenge. He'd been an asshole in the way he'd gone about it all, but I wasn't the confrontation type. If he didn't want me, then I wanted nothing to do with him.

I wasn't going to steal.

"No," I said.

"No?" she asked, standing.

"No," I repeated. "*Someone* stole all my money. I need this job."

"Exactly. Why clean for them when you can easily lift something they'll never notice is gone. You *need* to get something expensive and give it to me."

There were tons of expensive things in the mansion. Antiques. Paintings. Trinkets. Jewelry. I'd be able to pay for the exam I needed.

Except I wasn't like Paisley. I wouldn't take something that didn't belong to me, even if North hadn't bought it herself. This wasn't going to be a one-time thing. My "in" onto the Wainright property was the best thing ever in her mind. I did the dirty work. Figuratively and literally. She got the cash. It was better than shacking up with a guy. She didn't have to blow me.

No, she wasn't going to let this one go.

I shook my head. "Not happening. Get out, Paisley. Go find your two lovers and work your scheme on them. At least they get to fuck in trade."

I opened the door even wider. All the warm air had escaped and I shivered. She narrowed her eyes.

"This isn't over."

She stormed out and I slammed the door shut. I slid down it again, sat on the floor, tried to calm my racing heart. My hands shook and there was nothing I could do. I believed her when she said she wasn't done with me. Mexico wasn't enough. She didn't like to be told no. And my access to Wainright Ranch was too perfect for her to take a simple no from me and walk away.

I knew where I stood with the Wainrights. At least with South.

I had nowhere to turn. No one on my side.

I'd walked away from my mother and sister to start over. I'd known I'd have to do it myself. But in this moment, I'd never felt so alone in my life. What was the point in staying? Paisley knew where I was. I'd see South on occasion, probably with someone else. Could I handle that? I had nothing here but my job. Nancy was nice, but I wasn't kidding myself that I was irreplaceable.

Yet I needed the job. There was barely any money left at the end of the month after paying rent and food and everything else. And I needed the mammogram. What was I going to do?

10

SOUTH

THE MUSIC STOPPED. I shut off the torch, this hiss of the intense flame going quiet, and flipped up the welder's mask. Blinked.

West stood beside my huge speaker. It was connected to the Internet and pumped out whatever station I was in the mood for. Today it was heavy metal. Fitting.

"Jesus, how are you not deaf?" he asked.

I set down the torch, removed my thick gloves, then tugged off the mask.

"What are you doing here?"

West glanced around. "Where the fuck's your phone? Jed's been trying to get in touch with you."

"I've had my cell off since you left."

"That was three days ago."

I shrugged. Time blurred when I was working. And when I was trying to forget Maisey. I remembered showering, but I wasn't sure when. I'd hoofed it to my bed since the leather couch was out. Literally.

West had talked me out of setting the thing on fire, but he'd agreed to help carry it outside and to the back of the barn where I couldn't see it.

I focused on my project. Mostly. It was hard to get over Maisey being such a... guy.

She'd offered. Given promises. Shared falsehoods, a hard fuck. Then moved on.

Men did that shit to get in a woman's panties. Told her what she wanted to hear and after he bagged the babe, he went on to the next conquest. Forgot she even existed.

I didn't do that shit. I was a sad monogamous idiot who'd let a perfect ass and nerdy glasses distract me.

"What if she called?" he asked.

I rubbed my eyes, then met his gaze. He meant Maisey. "You were there. You saw her with those dudes. She wasn't selling them Girl Scout Cookies. Would you want her back?"

"Don't you want to hear what she has to say?" He tucked his fingers into the front of his jeans.

I continued to glare at him and he conceded. "Fine. You're right. I would want to burn the couch too."

"I'm fine," I told him. "Let Jed and North know. I'll surface sometime soon."

Eventually. I let a woman I'd been with for a couple of hours get under my skin, which was the most depressing part of this whole thing. I'd had one night stands before, but the woman had known the score. A one-time deal. A little fun, that was all. But Maisey—

"You'll surface now," he countered.

I took a step closer, suddenly on high alert. "What's happened? Is North okay? East?"

He raised his hand. "They're fine. I'm here to tell you—since Jed couldn't get through—that Maisey's been arrested."

I would have been less surprised if he'd said the zombie apocalypse was happening. "What the fuck?"

"Caught stealing at the big house," he explained. "Mrs. Sanchez called Jed and he hauled her down to the police station to scare the shit out of her."

Mrs. Sanchez was the housekeeper. She took care of everything inside the huge mansion. The cook, the cleaners. Repairs. It was her turf. She'd know if something had been taken.

I thought of Maisey alone and panicked in jail, then I remembered her cozying up to the two guys at the bar. "Why should I care?"

He shrugged. "Maybe you shouldn't after what we saw at the bar. Jed says something's not right though. Wants you there."

"Now?" My hands had little nick and cuts from my work. I was covered in soot and dirt. I probably smelled.

"Shower, then I'm driving. I'm not missing this."

———

MAISEY

"WHAT ARE YOU DOING HERE?"

I looked up, then froze at Nancy's words. My boss stood in her office doorway, arms crossed over her chest. While she didn't have a storefront, she had a small building that looked like a small converted gas station on the edge of town. She stored her van in the old service bay along with the cleaning supplies.

There was a small office to the side, which she stood in front of now, barring my path.

"I'm here to load up my supplies for tomorrow," I replied, my hands full with my cleaning caddies.

"I thought you were in jail," she said. Her voice held none of the warmth I was familiar with. Her arms were crossed over her chest and if it wasn't cold out, I'd think the wintry breeze was coming from her.

I blinked. Jail?

"Um... no."

She sniffed, then glared. "Well, if the Wainrights didn't arrest you, that's their prerogative. But if you think you still have a job after what you did, you must be dumber than a box of rocks."

What I did? I'd cleaned three houses today and had no issues. Nothing that would have me arrested or fired. My mouth fell open. Oh no.

"I trusted you, Maisey," she continued.

I could do nothing but stand there and let her scold me. I had no idea for what.

"Took you in when I thought you needed work. Desperate, you said," she continued. "What were you doing? Scoping out all the places?"

Her eyes narrowed and she stepped up to me, anger buoying her. "Did you steal from the others too? Things they haven't realized have gone missing?"

"What?" I asked, confused. "No!"

"I don't believe you." She pointed at me. If she stepped any closer, she'd poke my chest. "Probably everything you told me was lies. No money. Crazy family. I know crazy and it's right in front of me."

I swallowed hard. "I—"

I tried to get some words out, anything, but she cut me off. "I have to call all of my clients where you worked and tell them what you did. Apologize. Hope they don't drop me. Do you have any idea what your selfishness has done to me? My business?"

Oh.

Holy shit.

Tears filled my eyes. I knew what happened. It had been Paisley. She'd gone to Billionaire Ranch and stolen something. As me.

Nancy was right to be angry. What Paisley had done affected her business. Her livelihood. It wasn't just a trinket or a piece of jewelry or whatever it was that Paisley had stolen. Paisley thought billionaires wouldn't miss a few hundred or thousand dollars. But Nancy? This town was small. News of hiring a thief... me, would spread. Especially since her employees went into people's houses, often when they weren't there.

"I'm... I'm sorry," I whispered, setting the supplies

down on the pavement. I couldn't tell her it was my identical twin. Well, I could, but she wouldn't believe me, not now when she was angry. It was a far-fetched story. I'd tried to explain before in a similar situation, when Paisley had gotten me in trouble for something she'd done. It didn't matter anyway. I couldn't make this right, not when Paisley wasn't the least bit sorry. I didn't even know what it was she took, or if I could even get it back.

"There is no work for you in this town. If it hasn't already, I'll be sure to spread the news that you're no good. A thief. A liar. A swindler. Leave town. I never want to see your face again."

She spun on her heel and slammed the door shut behind her.

Tears streamed down my face. Paisley had done it. Ruined me.

I had no choice but to leave now. God, people would probably throw stones at me if I walked down Main Street. I had no doubt I would never get hired at any business in town, no matter the type of work. Probably the county. On top of that, I wasn't going to get paid for the past week's work. All that hard work and nothing to show for it. And Nancy thought the absolute worst of me.

God, so did the Wainrights. North and Jed were

probably mad. They'd been nice to me. Saying hello every time I saw them when I was working at their house. Making small talk. They didn't pretend I wasn't there. Or that I was the help, which was what I'd experienced in the past.

They trusted me and it was my fault Paisley had shown up. Had seen them as a mark. While she pretended to be me and use me for whatever she wanted often enough, I never imagined she'd steal from someone else. As far as I knew, I was the only one she took from. Now, my family's mess had touched the Wainrights.

Then there was South. Whatever his reason for not calling didn't matter now. He'd never want to be with me after he learned what I'd supposedly done. Sure, fucking a mousy house cleaner was one thing, but a thief? Never happening. Not after the little bit he'd shared about his father.

None of them deserved Paisley. I had to go, to steer her away. To protect them from whatever scheme she came up with next. She would plan something else, but I'd make sure it was far from South, North and Jed. All the Wainrights. If they knew I'd moved on, then Paisley couldn't remain either. Her cover would be blown.

I drove across town to my little house, swiping at

tears as I went. It was easy to pack. I only had the clothes and other few items I'd brought with me in July. None of the furniture was mine. Not even the dishes. I was packed within the hour and headed down the two-lane highway before the sun even set.

This time I had to go somewhere big, like Salt Lake City, where I could get lost and have plenty of job opportunities. Tucked in my purse I had the meager money I'd been saving from the job with Nancy.

With one hand on the wheel, I set my fingertips over my breast, felt for the little lump. Dread filled me. The cash was the start of what I needed to get checked out. Now I'd have to hope it would last until I could find someplace to live. Find a new job where no one knew me—or Paisley.

A new life. One where a handsome cowboy wouldn't call me beautiful. One where, for the first time, I hoped Paisley followed. I could at least save the Wainrights from me.

11

SOUTH

THE NICE THING about growing up in a small town was that everyone knew everyone. West and I said hello to the sheriff as he pointed us down the back hall to the observation room. Inside was Jed, drinking a cup of coffee. He leaned against the two-way mirror and eyed us. Jed had grown up here as well, even though he'd lived out of state working for the FBI since college. He had no jurisdiction to hold Maisey here, but I assumed it was a favor from a current law enforcement officer to a retired one.

I glanced from Jed through the glass to Maisey, sitting in the interview room at the metal table.

"Got 'em," West said, shutting the door behind us as if I was going to sneak out.

"Why isn't Smokey in here?" I asked, referencing the sheriff who was big and round and hairy. He'd had that nickname as long as I could remember. While it might be somewhat of a joke, the man was all business and a good officer.

"She's not under arrest," Jed replied.

I turned and glared at West. "That so?"

"North hasn't pressed charges," Jed explained, which made sense.

The big house was North's. As owner, she was the one who decided to have Maisey arrested or not. Jed wasn't her husband. He had no legal say in the matter, but I had no doubt if he told her to throw the woman in jail, North would take her man's advice.

"Then why are we here?" Seeing her sitting there, all fucking forlorn and shit, wasn't helping me move on.

"The Wainright name offers a few perks. I asked to bring her here to scare her straight." He glanced through the glass. "The Maisey I know would be panicking."

I stared at her. My heart did a flip. My fists

clenched and I wanted to not only go to her and wrap her up in my arms but throttle her.

She looked small sitting in the chair. Her arms were folded over her chest, her head tipped down as if looking in her lap. Her long hair curtained her face. I could see her eyes were puffy and her face red. She'd been crying.

I wanted to feel sorry for her, but then I remembered the cowboys licking lime juice off her chest.

"West said something was off," I said, glancing at Jed. He was far too relaxed with shit like this. Petty larceny was probably nothing for him. Of course, he also hadn't fucked the woman.

"Yeah. Take a look at her."

I flicked my gaze her way, then back at him. "I did."

"And?"

"And what?" I countered.

"I know you slept with her."

I turned and looked to West. "Are we going to braid each other's hair now too?"

He ran a hand over his neck. "He needed to know."

"Why the hell does it matter where I get my dick wet?"

"It's like that?" Jed asked. "I thought it was more serious."

I frowned. "So did I. I assume West told you about

seeing her at the bar." He nodded. I sighed. "I've spent the past three days trying to forget her. If this is to help me with closure, this little reunion wasn't necessary."

I gave Maisey one last glance. Tipped my head and studied her when she shifted, after tucking her long hair behind her ear and setting her hands on the table. Fuck, even sitting in a sterile interview room with the chance of being arrested looming over her, she looked good. I remembered how that soft skin felt. Tasted.

"Fuck," I growled, then left, Jed calling after me.

I made it as far as the lobby, setting my hat back on my head, before it hit me. What I saw.

I spun on my heel, pushed the door open. Jed and West looked my way. They hadn't even moved.

"That's not Maisey." I said, pointing at the woman in the other room. I set my hands on my hips and stared at her, trying to figure it out.

"I know," Jed said.

I whipped my head in his direction. "If you knew, why the fuck didn't you say so? Oh, you weren't going to tell me, were you?"

He looked at me as if he was dealing with a troublesome child. "You don't give a shit about Maisey Miles. You left."

"Why did you bring me here then?" I asked,

tossing my hands up. Since Maisey, or whoever the hell she was didn't look our way, the room was clearly soundproofed. I wasn't quiet.

"Because I thought you'd want to hear the truth," he countered.

I practically growled. "Fine. Tell me how you know that woman in there isn't Maisey."

"Tell me how you know it's not her first."

I stared at him, then ran a hand over my face. "Jesus. I didn't realize we'd returned to second grade. Fine. Maisey had a cut on her finger. She might have ditched a Band-Aid by now, but the cut would still be healing. Unless she's fucking immortal, there would be a wound."

Jed and West both looked at the woman's hands.

"I worked for the FBI for over twenty years," Jed said, giving his take. "I can read people. Unless Maisey has multiple personalities, that's not her. She's behaving nothing like the woman who's been in the house the past few months."

"And?" I asked.

"And our initial employee background check—"

"The one you said made her a good person," I cut in, reminding him of what he'd told me.

"—listed her having a mother and a sister, but we didn't look into them any further."

"She mentioned both," I said, remembering how much she hadn't liked either of them.

"She's an identical twin," West guessed, his voice filled with surprise.

What? "*What?*"

Jed nodded. "Paisley Miles. Same birth date as Maisey. Haven't fingerprinted her, but that would prove who she is."

"They're identical," West added, then frowned. "Wouldn't they have the same?"

Jed shook his head. "I looked this up online while I was waiting for you. While identical twins share the same DNA, they have different fingerprints."

"Then who did I fuck?" I asked, running a hand over the back of my neck. I'd fallen for the woman with the cut on her finger, but who was that? Maisey or Paisley?

"Time to find out," Jed said, moving toward the door. He glanced over his shoulder. "I assume you're staying?"

I glared and he gave a rare grin as he went out into the hall, then into the interview room.

Maisey—Paisley—sat up straight.

"Are you Maisey or Paisley?" Jed asked.

I watched as the corner of her mouth tipped up. Like she was pleased he was fooled.

"Not going to tell me?" Jed asked. "I can fingerprint you and we can wait for the results, which will take some time. You'll spend that time here in jail, at least a day or two, or you can tell me, and we can move things along."

She pushed her hair back, lifted her head and sniffed. As if she was favoring Jed with the answer. "Paisley."

"Want to tell me why you were stealing from the Wainrights?"

"Maisey made me."

"Holy shit," West whispered. We stood shoulder to shoulder watching this shit show through the two-way glass.

"She made you?" Jed repeated.

Paisley shrugged her slim shoulders. She wore the same outfit I'd seen Maisey wear. Her cleaning company t-shirt and jeans. Except her hair was down and she wasn't wearing glasses.

"She was the mastermind behind the whole thing," Paisley continued, clearly getting into the story. While her cheeks were tear stained, she seemed eager to share. "Scoped out the family. The house. Moved here and got a job with the cleaning company."

"You've been cleaning this whole time?" Jed asked.

Paisley looked shocked at the possibility. "No. I'm a

terrible housecleaner. I'd have been fired. She got the Wainright family's trust the past few months and then I was the one to come in and steal. Since we look the same, I could get in, no problem. She... she made me do the part that was against the law."

She made no indication she'd met Jed before, which jived with her story. Tears slipped down her cheeks.

"Oh, brother," West murmured.

Everything she said was spinning in my head. Maisey planning all this out. Using her sister for her dirty work.

"Where's Maisey now?" Jed asked.

Paisley shrugged. "No idea, but it only proves my point. I'm the one in jail and she's gotten away with it."

"Why didn't you do it in reverse if you didn't want to be caught holding the bag. Literally."

I had no idea what she'd tried to steal, but it had to be something to fit in a backpack or purse. It wasn't like she was able to sneak out my grandmother's grand piano.

"You don't know Maisey. She uses me all the time. Always has."

"You're saying you've done this before," Jed clarified, steering the conversation where he wanted it.

"I'm saying I want to tell you everything for immunity."

"You aren't an accomplice to a serial killer. This is petty theft."

"Are you sure that's all it is?" Paisley countered, leaning forward on her forearms. Getting closer to Jed and meeting his gaze head on. "I mean, she's had access to that mansion for a few months. Are you sure she hasn't stolen anything before now? I'm in jail and she's where?" She burst into tears.

I'd heard enough. I pushed out the door again and this time made it all the way outside. It was dark now and the air was sharp. Snow would be coming soon. West followed.

"Where the fuck are you going?" he called.

I ran a hand over my face again. "I have no fucking idea. All I know is that this mess doesn't involve me."

"You sure about that?"

"We had sex. I didn't marry the woman," I countered.

My cell rang and I pulled it from my pocket. "Wainright."

"South, hello. This is Nancy with the cleaning service."

"Hi, Nancy."

In the glow from the station's exterior lights, I saw

West's eyebrow go up. There was no one in the lot but us.

Since I'd have to repeat everything the woman said anyway because West was a nosey fuck, I pulled the phone from my ear and pushed the speaker button.

"I'm sorry it's taken me a little time to get to you, but I'm calling every client who's had Maisey Miles clean their homes."

"Oh?" I asked, meeting West's eyes.

I couldn't miss the woman's sigh. "I'm sure you have heard from your sister about the theft at her home, but I wanted to call you personally to apologize. Not only for having her steal from your family, but that I sent her to your house as well. I understand if you don't wish to use my services any longer after what one of my employees has done."

I caught on. I'd hired Nancy to have my house cleaned, specifically requesting Maisey, to get Maisey in front of me. My plan had worked. Too well.

I hadn't cancelled Nancy's services. I couldn't now because she'd believe I didn't have faith in her. This was a small town and I was a Wainright. If I ended my arrangement, others might as well. I wasn't an asshole, therefore it looked like I was going to have my house professionally cleaned from now on.

"It's not your fault, Nancy. Please have someone come at the same day, perhaps every other week?"

This time, when she sighed, I could tell it was in relief.

"I'll put you down. Thank you."

"Nancy?"

"Yes?"

"Do you know what Maisey's doing now?"

"Good question. I assure you, she won't be working in this town ever again. I told her to leave and never come back. I'm sure she's a hundred miles down the interstate by now. Good riddance."

Nancy hung up and I tucked my phone away.

West set his hands on his hips. "Maisey's left town and her sister's in jail."

"Paisley said she wasn't sure if Maisey had stolen things before now. If she took something small but valuable—"

"Which there is a lot of in that fucking house," West cut in to add. "How often do we go into the downstairs rooms? There's a Faberge egg in the den and I haven't been in there in... years."

When at the big house, I stuck to the kitchen and great room. The powder room right off of it. I hadn't been upstairs in forever. "Then she could be carrying a fortune, rolling out of town with her pride in tatters, but her sister behind bars."

"Holy shit. That's... cunning."

"Do you remember seeing a Band-Aid on the woman's finger at the bar the other night?" I asked.

West looked out into the dark as if trying to remember. "I wasn't paying much attention to her hands," he admitted. "Not when two men were practically sucking her tits."

I stepped away, spun in a circle and came back. My breath came out in a white cloud. There was no moon and the wind was sharp.

"I know for a fact I didn't have sex with the woman in there. If that's really Paisley, then I was with Maisey because of the cut. I marked her, too." I thought about how I'd sucked that dainty skin. "Gave her a fucking hickey. I'm not going to strip her down to check, but she'd still have a mark on her inner thigh."

Thankfully, West didn't comment on the fact I had my head between Maisey's thighs. "What are you going to do?" he asked.

I faced him. "Find Maisey Miles and learn the truth. I fucking hate liars. If she's guilty, I'm putting her behind bars."

"She isn't Macon," he reminded.

I stalled and my stomach churned. "No, but she's just like him."

"You sure about that? Trust your judgement, your gut. You had it bad for her. Things may not be as they seem."

"I intend to find out."

12

M AISEY

THE POUNDING on the door woke me. I popped up in bed and blinked, confused. Where was I? God, the crappy hotel. There was no clock in the room, but it was still dark out. Only the orange glow from the parking lot lights seeped through the cracks in the tired curtains.

The knock came again, and I jumped. "Maisey. Open the door."

South.

My heart was already in my throat from being

woken, but now I panicked. Why was South here? I was over three hours from his house.

Slipping from bed, I grabbed my glasses and put them on, then pulled the curtain aside and peeked out. The rooms of this old motel exited directly onto the parking lot. My old car was right in front.

There was South, staring at the door. The light hit him harshly, but with his Stetson on, his face was in complete shadow. I'd know him anywhere though.

"I'm not going away," he called.

While the banging had been loud, his voice was tempered down. Was it to let the others staying at the motel sleep or to keep from scaring me?

Either way, it was too late.

I heard someone shout through the wall to shut up.

I opened the door and South pushed his way in, forcing me to step back. I shut it behind him, the cold air making me shiver.

"What... what are you doing here?"

I hadn't seen him in person since I left his studio. Since he'd said he'd come to Billionaire Ranch to see me. My stomach flip flopped. I wanted to jump into his arms and have him hold me again. To tell me everything was going to be all right. Except he hadn't wanted me. Except—

He reached out, took a hold of my wrist and turned it as if he was looking for something.

I yanked against his hold.

It was barely light enough to make out his face. He flipped on a switch and the lamp—which had been put in this room in the late seventies based on the brass and orange shade—brightened the room.

I squinted, needing time to let my eyes adjust.

"Maisey," he said, running a finger over the cut that was slowly healing.

"What?" I asked, confused, yanking against his hold. This time, he let me go.

"Just want to make sure I'm talking to the right woman," he said, taking off his hat.

Oh.

He found out. *Of course* he found out. It was his family's house that had been robbed.

Realizing I was standing before him in just my panties and t-shirt, I grabbed the jeans I'd had on earlier, then sat on the edge of the bed to put them on.

"Don't do that for me," he said, his voice holding none of the warmth I'd heard until now. "I've seen it all. So have the guys at the bar."

I had one foot in my pants and looked up at him. I didn't like his tone, or his words. "What guys at the bar?"

He huffed and crossed his arms over his chest. "The two who used you as part of their tequila shots, then went with you to the bathroom to fuck."

"I... I don't know what you're talking about." I was catching on pretty fast though.

"Right," he scoffed. He didn't believe me.

"You met my sister," I said, returning to putting my pants on.

"Oh yeah." He crossed his arms over his chest. "You don't seem all that upset considering what happened."

I looked up at him. I wanted to argue. Fight for myself, what Paisley kept right on taking. She'd stolen South from me. He was a few feet away, but he wasn't mine. He hated me. His anger was pumping off him in waves.

I didn't have it in me. I was too worn down.

"I've been right here before," I told him. "A guy pushing me away because of Paisley."

"Pushing you away?" His eyes widened and he stared. "Are you fucking serious?"

I stood. I couldn't stay here a second longer in this shitty room with a guy who seemed to hate my guts. Even though it was the middle of the night, I wasn't going back to sleep. I'd keep on driving.

"I'm always serious." I stood, did up the zipper and the button. "That's the problem."

I didn't even look his way when I snagged a hoodie, then closed my bag. I grabbed it and my purse.

"Where the hell are you going?" He stared at me wide eyed, as if he expected me to take whatever shit he dished out.

"Salt Lake City. I'll have a better chance at finding work in a bigger place."

"Finding work or another family to scam?"

I spun on my heel and looked at him. My eyes widened and my mouth fell open. "You think—" I blinked, then took a breath. "What did Paisley say?"

"You're the mastermind." He came over to me, grabbed my purse from my hands. "That you set it all up and left her in jail while you run off with something valuable. What did you get? My grandmother's diamond brooch? The Faberge egg? That's going to be pretty hard to sell at a pawn shop."

We fought over my purse, but he was stronger. Going over to the tiny table, the laminate top worn and chipped, he tipped the items onto it.

"Hey!"

My cell, wallet, keys, a bag of tissues, lip balm and a tampon landed with a clatter.

He flipped open my wallet, read the ID. Then he rifled through it, tugged out the cash.

"Did you already pawn something?" His blue eyes met mine. They were ice cold.

I blinked back tears. I couldn't help it because he was digging through my things. Accusing. This was worse than learning Tommy had slept with Paisley. I shook my head.

He didn't believe me. He didn't believe *in* me. I'd learned long ago not to chase, to not try to run after someone who didn't want to be with me. I wouldn't be my mother begging for scraps from men who didn't give a shit about her. South definitely wasn't here because he wanted an "us."

"It's my money."

"There's got to be three, four hundred dollars here."

I might not beg for scraps, but I wasn't letting him take my hard-earned cash. He might have billions, but he held all that I had to my name. I reached for it, grabbed it from him and shoved it back in my wallet. I collected my things and slid them back in my purse. "It's all I have," I murmured, slinging it over my shoulder. "It's my word against Paisley." I looked South square in the eye. "You can believe me when I say I had nothing to do with what she did today. Or not.

Unless you've got a police officer out there to arrest me, I need to go."

"Running away." The words were tossed out as if they were foul.

I swiped at the tears that fell now. I *was* running away. From Paisley again. Yeah, her shit hurt, especially when I learned she'd said I was the mastermind, leaving her in jail. It was seeing South, knowing what he thought of me, that sliced deep.

I offered him a small smile and took one last look at the cowboy who I'd thought was mine.

"Yeah, running away. You've got it all figured out."

I opened the door, grabbed my bag off the floor and went to my car. There was no sense in locking it since no one in their right mind would steal it. I tossed my stuff in. It was fucking freezing.

"Maisey."

I looked up. He was silhouetted in the open room door.

"What?"

"Tell me."

"That I didn't do it?" I sniffed and wiped at my cheeks. "That it was Paisley? That she finally found me and used my access to a billionaire family as a dream come true? That she pretended to be me, again, so she wouldn't take the fall? That she blamed her scheme's failure on me, just like a sociopath does? It's what you want to hear, right? To absolve you or something?"

"Then why the fuck are you running away?"

I blinked and looked down the side of the motel. This was my life. Fleeing a cheap motel in the middle of the night. To nowhere. Anywhere.

"To protect you."

With that, I dropped into my seat and tugged the door closed with a squeak. Before South could move from the doorway, I backed out of the lot and drove away.

13

$\mathcal{S}$OUTH

I WENT into Maisey's hotel room and slammed the door shut. Sat on the edge of the bed, set my elbows on my knees. I picked up her familiar scent over a musty, mildew odor. This place may have been nice, back in the sixties. Now, it was rundown to the point of sketchy, built along an empty stretch of the highway. It was the middle of the fucking night and far from home. Hours from Billionaire Ranch.

Everything Paisley Miles at the police station had said had been accurate. Maisey had fled town. She had plenty of cash. I doubted North would press charges and Paisley would never step foot on the ranch again. We'd been duped. So had my dick.

I ran a hand over my face. Weary. Grabbing my cell, I called my sister.

"Did you find her?" she asked right away, even though it was four in the morning.

North had been a workaholic, pushing herself too hard. Then Macon had died and she'd met Jed. He helped with her work/life balance, sometimes even tossing her over his shoulder and carrying her away from her laptop and toward their bedroom. He dragged her to his off-the-grid cabin often enough. He didn't let her work there at all and she'd told me he stuck her cell in a kitchen drawer.

She'd been asleep, of course, although she sounded as if she was at her desk at the company headquarters in Billings instead of in her bed in the middle of the night.

I had to talk to someone, and it wasn't going to be West. He was more of a girl sometimes than North. Besides, chores on his ranch started early.

"Yeah. A motel close to the Idaho state line."

"And?"

"And she's gone."

"You let her go?"

"Why wouldn't I let her?" I countered, picking at a

fray in my jeans. "They stole... hell, I don't even know what Paisley Miles even lifted from the house."

"A bottle of Cognac."

"I could see Mrs. Sanchez busting her for taking anything from the house, but Jed thought she should be scared straight at the police station for a thirty dollar bottle of liquor?"

"Try a hundred thousand dollar bottle from the wine cellar," she countered.

Fuck. I'd pretty much forgotten it even existed. I didn't touch the fancy shit, sticking with whiskey or beer.

"It's a bottle of Cognac. Yes, it's a shit ton of money for a bottle of old grapes, but it's a *thing.* I'm more upset the woman's that cunning."

"I know," I replied. "And you didn't sleep with her."

Jed didn't keep anything from North. Since West had blabbed to Jed, North had to know about my thing with Maisey.

"Maisey? South, I was talking about Paisley," she countered.

"You don't think—"

"Jed and I agree. Paisley's the crazy one."

I sat up, stared at the old TV, the kind with the dial to change channels I remembered from when I was a kid.

"You pressed charges then."

"No."

I blinked. "I shouldn't have let Maisey go then? You want to arrest her instead?"

"No."

I wanted to sigh and growl and rip my hair out. "I'm so fucking confused. Why not?"

"Why did you go after Maisey?"

I had no idea why she was asking me this. If I were a kid, I'd respond with *duh*. Instead, I said, "Because she stole from us."

"We've had people steal before. This wasn't the first time and it won't be the last. Why did you chase after her? I mean, it's four in the morning."

"Because she *stole* from us," I repeated. Again, *duh*.

"Because you care," she countered. "You went after her because she took from you."

I did groan now. "I trusted her. Jesus, I told her she was the one. That I'd been waiting for her. Shit, I sound like I've grown a pussy."

North laughed. "It sounds like you found your heart."

I sighed, because I was so fucking tired and confused. Hurt and yeah, my heart felt like it had been back-kicked by a pissed off horse, then stomped on.

"What did you learn from her?" she asked.

"There's nothing hidden in her purse. She had some cash on her."

"That's what you found. What did she say?"

"That her sister's a sociopath. That she's moving to Salt Lake to find a job. To start over."

I heard Jed's voice, then muffling as it sounded like North covered up the phone, then she came on again. "You're on speaker. Jed's here."

It was the middle of the night. Of course he was there beside North.

"Hey," Jed said. "I'm thrilled we're doing this now, not hours ago at the station. You could've stuck around. Because of it, you're interrupting my sleep with my woman."

"He needs help," North told him.

"Princess, he needs to get his head out of his ass, is what he needs help with."

I wasn't sure why I was on the phone if they were going to talk as if I wasn't listening in.

"Fine, I bolted. Share your thinking," I told Jed.

"All you heard was what Paisley said. Took it at face value."

"Yeah, I believed her."

"An investigator has to hear what someone's saying, then break it down until all the puzzle pieces are put together in the right way. If you jam them in place, it doesn't make the right picture."

"Okay. Go for it, G-Man."

"Let's say Paisley is a sociopath as your woman says."

"She's not my woman," I countered.

He ignored me and continued. "Maisey moves to a new town, gets a job cleaning houses."

"Yeah, because she said her sister and mother used her and she was tired of it." I remembered her telling me this, especially because she'd been topless at the time.

"Paisley tracks her down and discovers Maisey's working for a family that's so loaded their place is called Billionaire Ranch. She likes get rich quick schemes and her sister's handed her one. Being identical comes in handy. She can pretend to be Maisey, get in the house without any issues at all and steal."

"If she got caught, she could say she was Maisey," North added.

"But we figured out she wasn't Maisey," Jed added.

They were on a roll, so I stayed quiet.

"She realizes she's in a pickle and spins the whole story around in her mind."

"In a pickle?" I asked.

He doesn't respond, just keeps going.

"Paisley got caught red handed. She was in the house under false pretenses. She was caught stealing an expensive as fuck bottle of Cognac. Maisey had nothing to do with it."

"So Paisley has to pass the problem onto Maisey," North added. She sounded excited, as if she liked this detective work. "Spinning a tale that Maisey's the one who set it all up. That she planned the whole thing for months. Made Paisley go in and pretend to be her so if Paisley got caught, she'd take the fall. Paisley even knew Maisey would leave town because she'd done it the last time Paisley worked her over, only a few months ago."

I stared at the shitty carpet and processed.

"You're saying Paisley's one fucked up woman and uses her sister," I said. "Found out where she was working and took it—us—as her golden ticket. But when it went south, she spun the story off of herself."

"Typical sociopath," North explained.

"I pulled their info," Jed added. "Banking. Credit cards. All of it."

"Being head of security for Wainright Holdings has some perks," I murmured. He'd quit the FBI right after he and North met and took up the job within the family business. I had a feeling it was because he felt personally responsible for North's safety and didn't trust anyone to do it. Twenty-four-seven.

"For once, I don't have to follow procedure," Jed countered.

"What did you find?"

"Maisey doesn't have a dime in her bank account. Checking or savings. It was emptied a few months ago."

"Right before she moved?"

"Yes. But hang on. Her credit card is maxed. She only has one of them and if she pays the minimum monthly payments, she'll be working to get out from under those for the next ten years. Her credit was frozen at the same time her bank account was emptied. Meaning no more cards can be added. Those maxed out charges include airline tickets to Mexico. A resort in Cancun."

"She went on vacation," I replied. "Yet she said she'd never been out of Montana."

"Maisey Miles doesn't have a passport," Jed added. "Passenger list includes a Paisley Miles and a male companion."

"Paisley used her sister's credit cards to go to Mexico with her boyfriend?"

"The bank withdrawal was the same day as the departure."

"She pretended to be Maisey and took her money out of the bank."

"We could pull bank cameras. Even cameras for the airport in Billings where they left from, but all it would show is—"

"A woman who looks exactly like Maisey," North added. "Oh my God."

"You're saying then that Maisey's exactly what she seems."

"Sweet, innocent, lost, determined?" North asked. "Totally fucked over by her evil twin?"

She was all those things. And more that she hadn't had a chance to tell me.

"That means—"

I worked through everything I'd seen and heard since I gave Maisey that last kiss in my studio.

"That means what?" Jed asked.

"That means the woman at the bar wasn't Maisey but Paisley."

"West said she picked up two men. That's in line with Paisley's personality. Mr. Mexico is probably long forgotten."

"That also means when she said it *can't* work between us instead of *won't*, she meant because of... holy shit," I said. "She freaked when I told her who I was. That I was rich. She was afraid to be with me because of my money."

"Because Paisley would eventually find out and do exactly what she did," North guessed.

I popped to my feet, starting to feel sick. And like a total asshole. "Fuck."

"What?" Jed said.

"Just now, I asked her why. Why she was running away."

"What did she say?" North asked on a whisper, sounding nervous about the answer.

"That she was protecting me."

Nancy had run her out of town. Maisey had no money, except for the cash she'd snatched back from me so protectively. She must have been afraid to open a bank account, her sister finding it and stealing from her again. *It's all I have.*

It literally was all she had.

Salt Lake would have jobs, but she'd have to survive on those few hundred dollars until she got a paycheck. There was gas, food, and she had no place to live. I glanced around at the hotel room. She couldn't even afford this shithole for long.

"Her sister can't pretend to be her any longer. Not at the ranch. Not in town," Jed said. "Even if news of her being an identical twin remains a secret, everyone will think she's Maisey and she'll be shunned." Jed's words made sense.

"Maisey is—and has been—Paisley's meal ticket. She'll follow her," Jed added.

"Away from me," I stated, beginning to pace the small room. "She didn't want to be with me because of Paisley. She'd avoided me because of that. I was pretty convincing though to make her mine."

I heard North's laugh through the cell. "I bet."

"She was right though. Paisley came, did just as Maisey expected. Except it doesn't seem as if Paisley knew about me and Maisey."

"No. I don't think she has any idea."

"Still, you got hurt," North added.

"I'm strong enough to—" I slapped the wall and a crappy picture tilted. A man through the wall yelled to shut up. "I got hurt. My heart's involved. North, what am I going to do?"

Maisey was out there. Alone. Broke. A sinister sister who looked exactly like her. She thought I hated her. I hadn't met her at the ranch as I'd promised, never even talked to her again until I showed up at this shitty motel. She hadn't just run away. I'd driven her off.

"Go get the girl. Then start groveling," Jed said, then hung up.

14

$\mathcal{M}$ AISEY

As if my life couldn't get any worse, my piece of shit car died. Steam started to come from the hood, or I hoped it was steam and not smoke, and I'd been able to limp to the nearest rest stop on the highway. I turned off the engine and the hissing and white plume from the hood stopped. But when I tried to start it again, it wouldn't even turn over.

Maybe I had a cracked radiator. No oil. A dead battery. There could be a clown beneath the hood fucking with the belts and hoses and I'd never know.

Dawn was breaking, a soft pink teasing at the sky

in the east. I was stuck at this rest stop until I figured out what to do. My only bit of gratitude was that I was better here than on the shoulder of the highway. I had a restroom and vending machines. There was money in my purse for a tow, but that would bleed me pretty much dry. I was in the middle of nowhere. It wasn't as if I could pick up a job in the middle of grassland and rock formations.

I was so tired. Tired of thinking. Of trying to get by. Of being used. Of... everything.

I closed my eyes. It was either give in to the exhaustion or cry some more. Grabbing my hat from the passenger seat, I tugged it on my head, then undid my seatbelt. It was going to get cold pretty fast without the heater.

I'd figure out the towing situation later, when it wasn't off hours and probably double rates. Sleep was all I could do. All I could handle. I closed my eyes.

A knock on my window made me jump and scream.

"It's me."

My heart was beating out of my chest as I realized it wasn't a serial killer waking me, but South.

Shit. I wasn't sure if the serial killer might be the better option.

I rolled down the window a few inches, thankful my car was so old that it didn't have powered controls.

"Are you okay?" he asked, his voice gentle, completely different than how it had been at the motel.

I pushed my glasses up and nodded. "What... what are you doing here?"

"Tracking you down. We need to talk."

The sun was peeking over the horizon now so I hadn't been asleep long. South wasn't wearing his hat and I could see his eyes were bloodshot and he needed a shave. His shirt was wrinkled. Behind him was his truck. I hadn't even heard him pull up and park.

"Why are you following me? I think we said everything earlier. I apologized. What else could you possibly want from me?"

He looked at the window as if it made him mad. "Open the door, beautiful."

"No. Go away, South. There's nothing left to say. Leave me alone."

"I tried that. It didn't work."

If he followed me from the hotel, then he wasn't going to just leave. I didn't have much choice. I could argue with him, but I was too tired.

I pulled up on the lock, pushed the door open.

South stepped back, then moved around into the opening and crouched down so we were eye level.

"Fine. What? I'm busy figuring out my next scam. You can tell by looking at my car and my thrift store clothes how well that's working for me."

He winced. "I was wrong."

"About what exactly? The fact that you don't believe in me? You're the one who told me to give us a chance and then after you got that *chance* you bolted? You ghosted me and made it very clear where I stood with you."

His jaw clenched, then he sighed. "After what we did in my studio, I went out with West and some friends to the bar on Main Street. I saw you there. You picked up two men." His blue gaze held mine.

I blinked. "Like I said, I had nothing to do with that. Sounds like Paisley."

He gave a tiny nod. "I thought you had your fun and had moved on."

I sucked in a breath, realizing what he must have thought. "No. God, I wouldn't have—"

"I was mad. Really, really pissed," he admitted. "Still am, I guess."

"South," I began but this time when he cut me off, he set a finger to my lips.

"I told you I'd come to the ranch and see you. I

didn't. I got drunk because I thought you'd tossed me aside. That what you told me were all lies. Just like the other women I told you about. Like my father."

I blinked, shook my head a little. "I thought you lied to *me*. That you used me. I felt just like my mother."

His eyes fell closed for a second. "Fuck, beautiful."

The air was cold and the touch of his finger was the only warmth I felt.

"You thought I was a liar, the one thing I hate most." I remembered what he'd told me.

I blinked back tears as I nodded, but they couldn't be stopped. "I'm... I'm so sorry."

He frowned, then lifted his hands and wiped my tears with his thumbs. "Why the fuck are you sorry?"

"I brought Paisley to you."

He cocked his head. "Did you?"

I nodded. "You told her where you were, that you knew of expensive liquor to steal?"

"That's what she took?"

"You've done nothing wrong." His gaze roved over my face, settling on my mouth for a moment. "I've been a fucking asshole to you. I believed Paisley's lies which made me an even bigger asshole."

"I am pretty mad," I admitted, still disappointed he'd thought the worst of me first.

"Jed said I'm supposed to grovel."

I didn't think South did that very often. If ever.

"I should have known," he admitted, taking my hand and stroking his thumb over the healing cut. "That it wasn't you at the bar."

"Identical twins fool everyone but their parents." I gave him at least that. "Sometimes even them."

"There's so much I need to explain about me being petty and shitty to you. I don't want to do it here. I need to grovel properly."

That made the corner of my mouth tip up.

"I'm so tired I can barely see straight. There are hotels a few exits back—nicer than the one you had—and we'll sleep. Then talk."

I stiffened. "I... my car's dead."

He looked to the dashboard, then back at me. His jaw clenched, realizing the situation. "You've had a pretty rough time, huh?"

The tears returned then because that was putting it mildly.

"What were you going to do if I hadn't come along?" he asked.

I shrugged, the lump in my throat making it almost impossible to talk.

"Come here."

He held his hands out in front of him and I didn't

think about the fact that I should be mad at him. That nothing had been resolved. Every single problem I had still existed.

Except he was offering me comfort and I needed it so fucking bad.

I turned and moved into his hold. He pulled me close, wrapping his arm about my waist, the other cupping the back of my head. He was warm. Solid. And he smelled like the South I remembered.

I cried then. Hard. I couldn't stop.

He stroked my back and whispered to me as I let it all out. I had no idea how long I wet his shirt, but the water works finally let up. I had nowhere to go. I wasn't sure if I believed South completely, but I was out of options. With the car dead and my money hemorrhaging, I had to get somewhere warm and safe first. I could worry about everything later. "We'll go to a hotel and sleep. After, you still have to grovel." I agreed with his plan, but wanted him to know everything wasn't resolved.

"All right, beautiful."

15

SOUTH

MAISEY WAS IN MY ARMS. She was so much smaller and it was a reminder of how fragile she was. Yet so fucking strong. The shit she had to carry on her slim shoulders would have crushed a weaker person. She was sprawled across me like a blanket, her leg between mine. Her head was tucked beneath my chin. I was warm and fucking content.

The only thing that would make this better was if we were in my bed, not a chain hotel off the highway, and if we were naked.

We hadn't talked after I'd tucked her into my truck at the rest stop, and once we'd checked into a room, only stripped off our shoes before climbing beneath the covers and falling asleep. Maisey had been on one side of the king-sized bed and I on the other. Like magnets, we hadn't been able to remain apart and I woke up with her like this.

In this moment, it was quiet. Everything was perfect. I had her in my arms.

But I didn't really.

Not yet.

All I was certain of was her safety. I had a feeling her car had driven its last mile. The fact that she'd been alone and stuck at a rest stop made me grit my teeth. She hadn't intended to call me for help. The fact that she'd checked into a run-down motel on the way to Utah instead of her mother's place in Billings told me how she felt about family. That she didn't have anyone to rely on.

I had to wonder what she would have done with the limited funds she had and her dead car. Would she have hitchhiked? If so, to where? Jesus, I didn't even want to imagine that.

I'd completely and totally fucked up. Jed had been right. She deserved me on my knees begging for her forgiveness because she'd fled in a shitty car with only a few hundred dollars instead of turning to me. The one she'd left to protect.

She stirred and lifted her head. She wasn't wearing her glasses and her dark eyes had that sleepy look. A crinkle marred her cheek, and her hair was tangled.

Perfect.

She turned her head away and covered her mouth with her fingers. I saw the healing cut on one. "I have horrible breath."

I chuckled. I hadn't even thought of that, but I probably could kill someone with mine.

"Let's shower," I suggested. "Then talk."

I had to make things right. I needed to seriously grovel until she forgave me. Gave us another chance.

I glanced at the bedside clock. Two in the afternoon.

She stiffened as if remembering everything that happened. "Yeah."

She shifted away and slid across the bed. I got up and waited for her to grab her glasses from the bedside table. I went around and held out my hand.

"You... you want to do it together?" The surprise and shyness in her eyes was endearing. And made my dick hard because when we'd had sex on my couch, it had only been her second time. The way she looked at me meant she'd never showered with a guy before.

Fuck. I had to will my hard on down because now wasn't the time.

"Hell, yes."

"This doesn't solve our problems," she murmured. "It doesn't fix my car or find me a job or deal with Paisley."

"No," I admitted, feeling like shit. Maybe this wasn't the thing to do. I hadn't been thinking. Still... "But it feels right."

Maybe she agreed. Maybe she wanted to get naked with me. Maybe she didn't have the energy to argue. Maybe she just needed a fucking shower. I wasn't going to ask her reasons for taking my hand and letting me undress her as the water heated.

She stood before me bare, all those soft curves on display, as she set her glasses on the vanity.

"Fuck, you're beautiful," I whispered, my words barely heard over the water. Her nipples hardened and goosebumps rose on her skin. I looked at her with such reverence, as if I couldn't believe she was allowing me this time. This closeness. I wasn't going to fucking blow it.

The Wainrights weren't emotional sharers. Growing up, my brothers, sister, and I had been stuck in a hell that didn't need talking about. We kept our shit bottled up. Only when Macon died did North tell us what she'd done. I doubted she'd have told us any of it if it hadn't been for Jed. He pulled the truth from her, helped her carry all that shit she'd handled on her own all her life.

I wanted to do the same thing for Maisey. Be her rock. The one she turned to. Not the guy she ran from. Or protected.

"In you go."

Only when the curtain slid closed behind her could I move. I stripped fast since my woman was naked and wet. I couldn't wait another second to join her. Taking the soap from her, I took my time lathering my hands, then using them on her skin.

"My father, Macon Wainright, was a dick," I said. My gaze followed my hands over her body, soaping up every inch of her. Talking about Macon kept my dick under control. It was the last thing I wanted to talk about, but I'd do it for her. Perhaps only her.

"He hated me and my brothers and sister. He'd yell at us. Talk shit. Laugh at our dreams. Call me and East and West pussies because of the dreams we had. Especially me, the oldest son."

Maisey remained silent as I talked. My body blocked the spray and I turned so the water rinsed her. Then I soaped her up again.

"I wanted to be an artist." I huffed out a sad laugh.

"*That* profession wasn't manly. Maybe being a ballet dancer would have been worse. Anyway, I heard it all. How all his money was wasted on me. How I'd be a pansy ass little shit artist. How I'd never make anything of myself because I was worthless."

She set her hand on my forearm and glanced at me but stayed quiet. I forged on.

"I heard it all. Took it all in. Obviously, it didn't stick since I went to art school and I'm a sculptor. I didn't know this until Macon died, but North made a deal with him so I could pursue my dream. She—" I paused, took a breath. "It still fucks with me, what she did. The fact that she'd kept it a secret made it even worse. She bartered me going to art school for her changing majors so she'd take over the business instead of what she wanted. The deals weren't for me alone. She kept Macon from breaking East's leg to keep him from playing football in college."

Maisey's gasp was heard over the water.

"Yeah, it was that fucking bad. The bargains she'd made. The sacrifices. He's gone. Six feet under. I told you I hated lies. Macon was the biggest one of all because while he touted being all manly, he was a closeted gay man. Not that being gay doesn't make someone a man, but it was the way he spun it. He was the biggest fucking hypocrite."

Maisey took the soap from me and ran it over my chest.

"Fuck, that feels good." My dick hardened and rose toward her.

"When I saw you... when I *thought* I saw you in the bar with those two men, it was a trigger. A huge fucking one. I bared my soul to you, and I thought you laughed at it."

"South," she murmured.

I stilled her hands, waited for her to meet my gaze.

"I should have believed in you," I admitted. "In this thing we have. Instead, I believed Macon. That I wasn't special or enough for you. I trusted a dead guy over you. I'm so fucking sorry."

She wrapped her arms around me, and I ripped them away. Dropped to my knees. The spray came over my head and trickled down my face. "No. I don't deserve your comfort," I snarled, angry with myself.

Her breasts were just above eye level. Full swells with plump pink tips. Her belly was smooth, her hips round and curvy. Leaning in, I kissed her navel, then the center of the little thatch of hair over her pussy. That was when I saw it.

My mark on her inner thigh. The one I'd made sucking on that delicate skin. Yeah, this was my woman.

I kissed it, licked the water from it. "This shows I was here. It proves we had something." I looked up at her, blinking away the water. "Will you share it with me again?"

"My pussy?" she asked.

My dick pulsed at her use of the naughty word. I couldn't help but smile.

"Definitely your pussy. But I want all of you, beautiful."

She set her hands in my hair, stroked it back. "Okay."

My eyes widened in amazement. "Okay? That's it?"

"That's it." She laughed and it was such an incredible thing. "My sister ruins everything."

I growled. "I also believed her over you. I'm sorry for that, too."

"She might not have a career, but she's really good at what she does."

I couldn't argue with that. "I don't want to talk about Paisley when I'm about to eat your pussy."

Her fingers tugged on my hair, pulled me into her. "Right. No talking."

Fuck, she was perfect. I licked into her and she practically ripped my hair out. It made my dick drip pre-cum. It would have to wait.

"No talking," I agreed. "Moaning and screaming my name are good."

I got to work then, nudging her feet a little farther apart, as far as the hotel's tub would allow, and I licked and sucked every bit of her soft pink flesh. Her flavor coated my tongue and my only goal in life was to make her come. I hooked her leg over my shoulder to open her nice and wide.

With a finger curling inside her and my tongue flicking at her clit in the way I was quickly learning she liked best, she writhed and called out my name.

When her inner walls rippled and I knew she was close to coming, I pulled back, sat on my heels.

"No!" she cried. Her eyes flew open. "Why... why did you stop?"

She looked down at me and blinked.

"I might be in the fucking doghouse, but woman, you said you left to protect me."

Her fingers loosened on my hair. "What? I... If I went away, Paisley couldn't bother you anymore. She couldn't pretend to be me. She had no con. She'd go away. Or at least follow me."

"Beautiful, if you ever want this pussy licked again, you'll stop that shit right now," I growled.

"South, I—"

"I mean it. You think I can't protect my family? You?"

"She *stole* from you."

"Things. She took a bottle of liquor." I wasn't going to tell her the value. "We might have more money than Midas, but my siblings and I don't give a shit about the money. We learned the hard way that people are what is important. Family. She almost stole *you* from me and that's not fucking okay."

"She's not going away. She'll always follow me. Always use me." She sounded so beat down over it.

I shook my head and water slid down my cheeks. "Your man is South fucking Wainright. You think I can't handle her? I've also got a kick-ass sister, two ruthless brothers, and an ex-FBI agent on my side. Oh, and a billion dollars."

A smile slid across her face and her fingers tugged at my hair.

"Okay," she whispered.

"Okay? You'll stop protecting me?"

"You'll start eating me out again?"

I grinned. "Beautiful, try to get me to stop."

16

MAISEY

"WANT SECONDS?" North asked, holding up the bowl of mashed potatoes.

"I'm stuffed," I said, leaning back in my chair.

Out of the corner of my eye I saw South smirk. I glanced at him and he waggled his eyebrows. His mind was certainly on me being *stuffed* a different way at the hotel earlier.

I blushed. Of course. I quickly looked around the table at West, North, and Jed to see if they noticed. West was grabbing the platter of meatloaf, using the spatula to put another helping on his plate, focused on satisfying his stomach.

The way they attacked the meal, it was clearly a favorite their chef made.

We were at Billionaire Ranch. At the kitchen table, which seated eight, had a seasonal floral arrangement in the center—different than when I was here last— and was tucked in a breakfast nook. I knew first-hand the view that was out the window was impressive, but it was dark now. After the shower, South had dragged me back to the bed, unable to keep himself away from me. Unable to keep himself *out* of me until house-keeping knocked on the door. We'd checked out and drove the few hours back to the ranch for dinner.

He'd wanted to drive right on past to his farm-house, but North had all but forced him to dinner. They wanted to make sure Maisey knew they believed in her, that they held no hard feelings and that North had called Nancy to tell her what had happened.

They were helping to make things right, even though they were the ones wronged. It felt good to know they were on my side, but it was awkward.

South took my hand under the table, set it on his thigh. "You okay?" he whispered, his eyes only on me. He'd barely stopped touching me since he found me at the rest stop. I liked it. A lot. As if he could never get enough of me.

Especially right now because I was a little uncomfortable and it obviously showed. "I... um, this is a little weird for me. I mean, I cleaned this floor the other day. Now I'm eating here." I glanced around the beautiful kitchen.

North had been my client. Customer. No. I'd scrubbed her toilets, emptied her trash cans. Even though they were welcoming and the truth had come out, I was still the minimum wage employee who'd been fired for stealing from her.

"I mucked stalls this morning. Hopefully I don't smell like shit," West said, then gave me a wink. Just like South when I'd first met him, he didn't look like a billionaire. I was coming to realize they didn't have a specific *look,* at least not in Montana.

"We'll keep saying it. You're welcome here," North said. She was in pink fleece pullover and sweats. Her sleek hair was pulled back in a simple ponytail, and she wasn't wearing any makeup. "I wanted to make sure you knew how we felt. We're all used to crazy family members and certainly are the last people who would blame someone else for another's actions. Besides, I'm thrilled you're with South." Her eyes sparkled. Under that usual hard exterior she showed, here at home she was a romantic.

Jed nodded. "You're an interesting case."

North poked him in the upper arm. "She's not a case."

"She's not a fucking case," South added, clearly put out. "Just like North wasn't a case for you the second you laid eyes on her at the wake."

Jed's jaw clenched, but when he glanced at South, he relaxed. "Fair point. Except I never had an evil twin in all my years at the FBI."

I couldn't help but laugh. "Evil twin. That's good." It was definitely a good description for Paisley.

"Now what?" West asked, scooping up some peas. "Have you heard from your sister?"

I glanced around, settled on Jed. "I haven't, but you've seen her since I have. I don't know what she told you. I don't understand why you didn't have her arrested."

Jed crossed his arms over his chest. His dog came over and nosed his elbow. Jed stroked his ear as he said, "Even though the Cognac was... expensive, she'd probably only get community service and we figured you didn't want her sticking around to perform it. Besides, consequences have no real impact on sociopaths. They have little morals or remorse."

I had to agree with him. While he didn't know Paisley as I did, I was sure he'd dealt with plenty of people like her in his former job. "I think you're right. Only the chance of a long jail term would scare her, and she wouldn't get that from her past activities."

"Still, I shared some not-so-subtle threats before I let her go."

"She's not done," I warned. I'd told South the same thing back at the hotel, but he'd distracted me. Very pleasantly. Just because we didn't talk about it didn't make the problem go away.

"Here at the ranch she is," Jed countered, his voice deep and serious. Deadly even as he leaned over and kissed North's brow.

I stood, grabbed my empty plate and carried it to the kitchen sink. I set it there then went back for the other dishes.

South stood, towered over me. "What the hell are you doing?" he asked when I grabbed his plate.

"Dishes."

He took the dish from my hand. "West does them. Or I do. If someone else cooks, we clean. No matter who does the cooking here."

"Well, someone else cooked for me, so I'm going to clean," I countered, skirting around him.

"You don't work here any longer."

I stilled. Fuck.

One sentence and it was like a bucket of ice water was dropped on my head. What was I doing? I didn't have a job. My car was dead, still sitting at the rest stop. I'd paid rent on my apartment for the rest of the month, but had no money for it after that. I'd already cleaned all my stuff out. I was pretty much homeless, or soon would be.

"I don't work anywhere."

"You don't need a job if you're with me." South was serious and that had me freaked. I grabbed the plate, set it back on the table, then tugged him into motion.

"Excuse us," I called, as West still shoveled meatloaf into his mouth. Since I knew the layout of the house, I pulled him into the small room beneath the stairs, flipped on the switch, then shut the door behind us.

"You want me alone, beautiful?"

"Yes, but not for what you think." I leaned against the door. While I had no doubt South could pick me up and move me to get out, I felt as if I had his attention. "I need to work."

"No, you don't."

"Yes, I do." I wasn't telling him about the mammogram.

I sighed, closed my eyes for a second, then opened

them. Tipping my chin back, I pushed up my glasses. "South, I won't be beholden to you."

"Beholden?"

"I won't have you taking care of me like a... like a sugar daddy."

A slow, sly smile crept across his face. "You want to role play? If that gets you hot."

I pushed at his chest, not to move him because that wasn't going to work. "South! I mean it. I have no money except for the cash in my wallet. My car is dead at a rest stop. I have no job. A place to live for only another week or so. I *need* money and soon."

"I'm aware of all that. You'll move in with me."

He made it sound so easy.

"And then what?" I wondered.

"Then I'll be your sugar daddy and I'll turn you over my knee for being a bad girl."

My mouth fell open and my nipples got hard.

"You like that idea." He moved closer, which wasn't much since this weird room was so small. I smacked his chest again.

"I won't be like my mother. I won't be reliant on a man. If something happens then I'll be... God, out on the streets."

Any hint of a smile slipped from his face. "Oh. You

want to work for Nancy still? North explained the situation. I'm sure she'll take you back."

"Maybe. I need to be independent. I need to get my life back on track." He wanted to house me and feed me and... God, I wasn't going to add my healthcare onto all that. Then I would be even more dependent.

"What track was that?" He dropped into the little corner seat so I didn't have to get a crick in my neck to look at him. He hooked a hand behind my back, pulled me close so I stood between my knees.

"I was in college. I have about a year to go. I had to drop out."

"Why?"

"Because of Paisley. That money she stole and used for her trip to Mexico and whatever else it was she bought on my credit card?"

He grunted. His eyes narrowed and if smoke could come out of his ears, it would be right now. "Let me guess. Tuition?"

I nodded.

"What were you studying?"

"Nursing."

He smiled again, this time softly. He leaned in and kissed me. "I can see that. You want to finish? I'll pay for it."

"South, I can't—"

"You wouldn't be shacking up with a guy expecting him to support you financially."

"That's exactly what I'd be doing. Shacking up with you."

He shook his head. "No, beautiful. It'd be your man giving you what you needed to get ahead. I'll say it's me being selfish."

"How is that?"

"There just so happens to be a hospital nearby. And doctor's offices. Even some schools who need nurses. You want to work and support yourself, then do it with a career you love. Get your nursing degree and then you can come home from a day helping people and your man will be waiting to bend you over the couch and claim your pussy."

I couldn't help but melt into him. Smile. Become aroused. "Pervert."

"Don't tell me you're not wet thinking about the possibilities. Besides, I have the money," he continued. "Let me spend it on something worthy. You."

"South," I sighed. I understood his perspective, but I was too sensitive now. After what Paisley just did and my mom's man trend? I was petrified to rely too much on him and then be right back where I was this morning. In a broken car with only a small amount of money.

"It's settled then. You're shacking up with me. Going back to school. Getting well fucked."

"It's not as simple as that. I worked full time and went to school."

"It is as simple as that. We're a team now. You see Jed and North. You think they care about the money differences?"

I shrugged. "I have no idea."

"But you see how into each other they are. That's serious love."

"Jed might not live there, but I know he has his own place. Money from the FBI. Retirement accounts. I don't have any of that," I countered.

"There's nothing wrong with relying on someone, beautiful."

"I couldn't rely on my family," I admitted. The people who I should've been there for me. What if the lump was more than a lump? I tried not to panic about it, but how could I not worry?

I didn't see pity in his eyes, only understanding. "I couldn't rely on Macon and I did what I wanted anyway. I had the Wainright money to support me, for which I was lucky. But working full time and going to nursing school is crazy. I'd like to see you sometime when you're conscious, beautiful. I'm selfish."

I pursed my lips because I had run myself ragged. "Greedy, more like it," I murmured. "Fine, I admit the idea of your plans for the sofa have merit, but there's still Paisley."

He growled. "Jed said he threatened the shit out of her."

"She doesn't scare easily," I reminded him.

"She can't hurt us again."

"You sound so sure of yourself," I said, studying him. He looked as if he'd resolved something in his mind.

His blue eyes met mine. Held. "I am. I love you, Maisey Miles. I want you. Only you."

"Wh—what?"

"I told you I wanted an *us*. Maybe I got derailed, but I haven't changed my mind. Never will."

"I... I—"

"You what?" he asked, no more than a whisper.

"I don't know how, but I love you too." My heart swelled, filling all the empty and alone spaces. Things were unsettled. Unresolved. Yet I felt like we could conquer anything together.

He pulled me into him. Kissed the hell out of me.

"We need to trust in what we have. What we'll build together. No one will pull us apart."

He was serious. The blue in his eyes was filled with intent. Heat. Need. Love.

"Okay. Trust." I didn't realize how soon it would be tested.

$\mathcal{S}$OUTH

WE GOT A DAY OF QUIET. A day of being alone with Maisey at my farmhouse. No interruptions. I ditched my projects. All we did was stay in bed and fuck like rabbits. I barely let Maisey get dressed, and then only in my flannel and a pair of thick socks. Nothing else. If she was cold, I warmed her. If I needed her again, I flipped up the long tail of my shirt to get inside her.

It was perfect. I understood why Jed had his cabin in the woods. Why he'd originally tossed North over his shoulder and took her there. He wanted North all to himself and he knew how to do that. She was a workaholic but had a reason now to leave at five.

Maisey worked her tail off for money, living fucking hand-to-mouth. I wanted her to have a chance to make her mark on the world and she'd do that once she had her nursing license. She'd finally be able to get ahead, to support herself. To get ahead. While we'd be married—yeah, she didn't know about that plan yet—I'd ensure she had a bank account only she could access. No one else, including her sister. That way that part of her hurt soul would know she'd always be able to stand on her own, even though she'd always lean on me.

She wouldn't be doing nursing school or anything alone again. I'd be right there with her, every fucking step of the way.

The doorbell rang and Maisey rolled over and groaned. It was ten in the morning, not very early, but I'd kept us up late. I saw the slight pink marks on her wrists where I'd used some old ties I only wore for weddings to restrain her to the headboard. My dick got hard thinking about how she'd writhed and screamed.

We were working through a number of my fantasies and finding out a few of hers. Turned out, my shy girl was into a little kink.

"It's probably West. I'll kill him and then he won't bother us anymore," I said, climbing from bed and tugging on my jeans.

I glanced out the window. The weather was shit, the mountains socked in with clouds. It had rained overnight and now snow threatened. The perfect day to stay in bed and show my woman the fun in a little ass play.

"Go back to sleep, beautiful. You're going to need it," I said, patting her upturned ass beneath the blanket. She mumbled, then rolled over.

I swore as I stomped down the steps. "West, I swear, you need to find your own fucking woman."

I yanked open the door, ready to kick my brother in the balls.

It wasn't West, but Micah Cunningham, the misogynistic asshole who'd come to the studio to talk about a sculpting commission. Beside him was Paisley.

Fuck me. The last two people I wanted to see. Together.

Maisey had been right. Paisley wasn't going to stop.

"What the fuck do you two want?" I snarled.

Cunningham grinned, then pushed his way inside. He had on his motorcycle-chic outfit of black jeans and another black t-shirt beneath a canvas vest, although I doubted he owned a Harley. He'd shaved since he'd been here last. Even got a haircut, but it didn't make him look clean-cut. You couldn't take the asshole out of this guy with a trip to the barber. "This place for one, but serious upgrades are needed."

I didn't want to close the door, but it was fucking freezing out. After shutting it, I stayed right where I was, making it clear they weren't welcome. They took in the living room as if they were at a Sunday open house.

"What the fuck are you talking about?"

Paisley took in my bare chest. "I see why Maisey's into you. When Micah first told me she was your woman, I almost laughed in his face. She's smarter than I thought. She might want your body, but we're here for your inheritance," Paisley said, flicking her hair back. Fuck, she looked just like Maisey. The resemblance was scary. The only difference I could tell —besides the attitude—was the lack of glasses and the taste in clothes. She wore jeans and black boots, which was neutral enough, but I doubted Maisey would wear something as flashy as the hot pink puffy coat.

"My inheritance?" I asked her. "You want money."

She nodded as her eyes darted around. "You're right, Micah. This isn't as grand as Billionaire Ranch, but it will do."

"Turns out, I didn't have to keep my eyes off your woman. I found one who looks just like her all on my own," Cunningham said. "I bet mine's wilder in the sack."

Paisley giggled and ran her hand down Cunningham's arm. "Imagine his surprise at the bar when he discovered we were twins?"

"Imagine that," I grumbled. "At the bar on Main, I'm guessing." She changed men like most women changed underwear.

She nodded.

"Paisley did what? Sucked your dick for your help to extort me?"

"Oh, she sucked my dick, but for the chance to get her hands on a shit ton of money. We both want revenge."

"Revenge for what?" I asked, internally rolling my eyes.

"Maisey got the man and the money," Paisley said with a pout. "She should share. Instead, she sicced that... that bearded asshole on me."

Jed was a bearded asshole, to everyone but those he cared about.

I looked to Cunningham. "What about you? You want revenge because I wouldn't make a sculpture for you?"

"No. Because you got Macon Wainright's inheritance. It's mine."

"Why the fuck is it yours?" I asked, tired of the pair.

"Because little brother, he's my father."

Cunningham was Macon's kid? Holy shit.

"My mother told me," he explained. "There are pictures of her with Macon. They were lovers. In love."

Obviously he didn't know Macon's secret. Perhaps Macon had been bisexual instead of gay. Perhaps Micah's mother was a beard, a way to hide his homosexuality.

"We'll get you a DNA test," I said. I'd rather see the money be donated to a charity like I'd told North to take care of, but if he was Macon's, Micah could have it. I didn't want a dime.

"There is no *we*," he snarled, pulling a gun from his jacket.

Paisley gasped and jumped back. "Micah!"

I froze.

"You're going to die and I'm going to be the only legal heir. The money will be mine."

"Micah, we didn't say anything about killing," Paisley said. Her eyes were wide and she held her hands up in front of her. It was obvious she wasn't in on this. Or she deserved an Academy Award.

He laughed, flicked a glance at her then back to me. "We won't have as much if we have to share it. Now, where's that identical twin hiding?"

Like I was going to tell a gun-toting asshole where my woman was?

"Go find her," Micah told Paisley, waving his gun.

Paisley took a deep breath, then cut through the rooms on the main floor. The house wasn't huge, so she was done quickly. She went up the stairs. I wanted to grab her, yank her back, but I didn't know what she'd do. Or who Cunningham would shoot first. All I knew was that Maisey was in the house, and I'd do anything to keep her safe.

————

MAISEY

"Sissy, wake up."

I startled and popped up. "What are you—"

"Shh," Paisley said, putting her finger over her lips.

She looked to the door, then grabbed my glasses off the bedside table and handed them over. "You have to listen to me."

"Well?" A deep voice shouted from downstairs. Not South.

My eyes widened at the growl in the one word. "Who's—"

"Found her. She has to get dressed!" Paisley yelled back. Her gaze met mine again. "I'm sorry," she whispered. "I only wanted the money."

I sat up and the bedding dropped. I was naked, but I didn't care. What I had, Paisley had.

"Start at the beginning."

She glanced at the closed door. She must have shut it after she came in. "I met a man at the bar when he thought I was you. Said he'd been here scoping out the place when South got all caveman protective of you. I knew you cleaned Billionaire Ranch, but I didn't know you hooked up with South. Not until he told me. This guy, Micah, he says he's South's half-brother. Macon Wainright's son. We decided to work together to get his inheritance. I mean, it's his if he's Macon's son. But now that we're here, he plans to *kill* South to get all the money."

My eyes widened and my heart rate skyrocketed. "Kill him? South only found out recently he's Macon's child. How does this guy know?"

Paisley shrugged and her coat rustled.

"Why go after South? Why not the others?"

"I guess because of me. You. Us." She waved her hand in the air. "He *hates* South. He said he got tossed off the property for no good reason."

No good reason? He'd been a dick. The guy really was an asshole. But a dangerous one. Shit. "He's downstairs now?" I hissed.

She nodded, then glanced at the door. "He's got a gun. I'm so sorry. I don't know what to do."

"Where's South?"

"With Micah."

South had a gun on him. I had to save him. I climbed from the bed and grabbed South's flannel off the floor and put it on. Then I went to the dresser and pulled out clothes. I didn't have much, but South had insisted I tuck them away instead of living out of a bag. This was my house now, he'd said.

If that was the case, then I protected what was mine.

"You came here with him?" I asked. "I mean, he didn't force you?"

She shook her head. "No. I had no idea he was this crazy until now. We met—"

"At the bar. Like you met two men earlier in the week?" I asked.

She didn't flush but glanced away. Now wasn't the time to scold her.

"I only wanted the money." She came over to me, took my hand and squeezed. "I'd never *kill* anyone. I'm sorry, sissy."

It seemed there actually was a line in the moral sand that my sister wouldn't cross.

"You're only sorry because it's gone out of control," I snapped. "The fact that you were willing to help extort money out of a stranger just because he's loaded? You slept with a guy who'd do that?" I shook my head, not understanding her value system. "Why didn't you go to the police?"

Tears wanted to come and my hands shook, but now wasn't the time to panic. I couldn't.

"It was only supposed to be about the money," she whispered.

"When I go downstairs, what do you think he's going to do with me?" I glared at her and her eyes widened, obviously not having considered that.

"I wish I was more like you."

I wish I was more like you.

"I have an idea," I said, knowing instantly what had to be done. I looked her over and grabbed my jeans from the drawer. "Take off your jacket and boots."

"What?" She frowned, cocking her head to the side in the exact way I did.

"You wanted a chance to be like me," I murmured, grabbing socks. "Now you've got it."

"He's going to kill me instead of you."

"Are you fucking kidding me? You brought him here," I spit out, shoving my foot into my jeans. "If you can't sway him, then I will. Give me your fucking coat."

Awareness, perhaps at the size of the clusterfuck she'd gotten us into, lit her eyes and she nodded, quickly doing as I instructed.

If this was going to work, whatever ended up happening, we had to be convincing. I didn't have to worry about Paisley. She'd spent her entire life pretending to be me.

18

 OUTH

PAISLEY CAME DOWN the steps first, Maisey right behind. It was the first time I'd seen them together. It was fucking freaky how much they looked alike. If I could give them closer scrutiny, I hoped I'd know which one was mine other than knowing Paisley had on a hideous coat and Maisey wore glasses. I couldn't though, not now.

Every molecule of my body was primed to protect my woman, but Cunningham was twitchy and I didn't want to set him off. Not with Maisey anywhere near that gun. She ran over to me and I wrapped my arm around her waist and pushed her behind me. It wasn't much, but I was reassured she was a little sheltered.

"You girls are going to stay here together while Wainright and I head to his barn. Too bad the acety-lene tanks are going to blow and hide the fact that you were shot in the head."

"What?" Paisley screeched.

"No!" Maisey cried at the same time, gripping my side.

Those tanks were safe, if kept stable. I had them securely fastened together and against the wall and the space was temperature controlled. If the gas leaked and there was a spark, the whole building would blow when all the tanks ignited. Cunningham was right. No one would suspect a bullet to the head because I'd be a pile of ash.

"Once I've taken care of your boyfriend, you're coming with me." Cunningham pointed at Maisey. "I've always wanted to fuck twins."

"Over my dead body," she snapped.

"That is an option." Cunningham's eyes were narrowed and I didn't even want to contemplate why his dick was hard.

"I'll do it," Paisley announced, looking my way. Assessing. She lifted her chin and sniffed, then glanced at Cunningham. "I'll kill him. You'll have an alibi, Micah. I mean, no one would suspect you of the fire if you're not here. An accidental gas leak and explosion is what will be found. And since Maisey will be seen with you, everyone will think she's me, meaning I'll have an alibi too. I'll use Maisey's car and meet up with you. We'll both be in the clear."

Yet they'd have an extra Paisley-lookalike walking around who knew the truth.

Cunningham's eyes flared with interest and didn't pick up on the flaw. Or several of them. Obviously they didn't know Maisey's car wasn't even here. If Paisley left in my truck, that would be a red flag. It wasn't like she could walk to town from here. Not in this weather.

On top of all that, I had to wonder how Paisley knew what an acetylene gas tank was or even used for. Since they'd come here because of Macon's money, she had to know Cunningham had scoped me out the other day as a prospective client. She was in on this whole scam.

I didn't like her based on everything Maisey had shared, but I'd taken her for a shallow, vain, remorseless woman. Not a killer.

"I didn't figure you to be more than a quick fuck, but I was wrong," he told Paisley.

Maisey's fingers clenched my bare upper arm at

his words. Paisley's smile slipped a little, but a shrug showed she didn't care. "I'm always underestimated."

"This is bullshit," I swore. "All of this for Macon's money?"

Cunningham raised the gun and shot a hole in my ceiling. Maisey screamed. Paisley ducked, covered her head with her hands. I flinched and pushed Maisey further behind me. "Says the cowboy who has all the cash in the world."

"I'll fucking give you his money. You want it, you can have it. Just leave Maisey alone." I was sick and tired of Macon ruling my life. Because of him, I had a guy shooting up my house, endangering my woman. I'd found Maisey—and groveled to get her back—and now this asshole wanted to fuck her along with her twin sister? Yeah, not fucking happening.

"I'll get it," he vowed. "My mother worked two jobs to make ends meet and never saw a dime from him before she died. She earned that money and so did I. I wore second-hand clothes and ate macaroni and cheese and bologna sandwiches. I'm getting every penny that's rightfully mine. When you're dead."

Paisley recovered from his insults. "Give me the gun. I'll do it."

Cunningham shook his head. "Not happening. I'm

not getting shot in the back." He tipped his head toward the back of the house. "To the barn. Move."

I didn't have a choice but to go. I set my hands on Maisey's shoulders and kept her in front of me. If he wanted to get her, he'd have to get through me first. I was only wearing my jeans and it was fucking freezing. The ground was cold and rough beneath my bare feet, but I didn't feel any of it. My adrenaline was pumping. I leaned down, whispered in Maisey's ear once we were outside. "It's going to be okay, beautiful."

Her shoulders stiffened, but she kept on walking.

When we were at the barn, I didn't open the door or go inside, not getting anywhere near the tanks that fueled my welding work.

"Micah. Go," Paisley said, stepping close to him and pressing her tits into his arm. Even through her thick coat, he no doubt felt her rubbing them back and forth. "I'll take care of this. Give me the gun."

"How do I know you aren't going to shoot me?" he asked, eyeing her with suspicion.

"Because if you're dead, I can't get any of the money, now can I?" She idly played with his ear lobe.

He grunted, then cupped her hip. Stroked it. "That's right."

He looked down, tugged on her shirt that hung beneath the pink coat. Stared at the plaid.

A plaid I recognized as mine. The one she'd been wearing the past day and nothing else...

Cunningham lifted his gaze. Narrowed his eyes. "You're not Paisley," he snarled and raised his free hand. The one with the gun.

Holy fuck.

If she wasn't Paisley, that meant... I wasn't protecting Maisey. I was shielding the wrong fucking sister with my body.

He grabbed Maisey. Yes, Maisey. I couldn't see Maisey's hand or the cut the way her body was turned, but the look on her face was panic.

Cunningham was distracted and I launched myself at him. He swung his arm out and caught me on the shoulder, knocking me sideways. The gun fired and hit the barn behind me.

Maisey jerked away, fell to her knees, then popped back up and started to run away.

I watched as Cunningham turned toward Maisey and raised the gun again.

He wanted me dead. Yet he was aiming now out of reflex. Anger.

"No!" Paisley yelled, running toward Cunningham. All of a sudden, she was like a whirling dervish, an angry mama bear protecting her cub. Something. Any description of a woman who'd lost her shit. I grabbed Cunningham by the arm as Paisley launched herself at him like a wrestler in the WWF. The gun fired and Paisley screamed, then fell to the ground.

I grabbed Cunningham's wrist with one hand, punched him in the face with the other. He slumped, but rebounded.

"No one."

Punch.

"Fucks with."

Crack.

"My woman."

Spurt.

The gun fell to the ground and Maisey dashed for it. Grabbed it. I didn't stop beating the shit out of Cunningham. I was fucking pissed and I had to let him know that he was not the winner here.

Only when he slumped, unable to remain standing did I release him. He hit the ground hard, unconscious. His face was bloody. His nose was definitely broken. So was his right elbow and wrist. Maybe even a rib or two.

I wanted him dead, but a few decades behind bars would be fine too.

"Paisley." Maisey crawled over to her sister who

was laying on her side, her hand over her shoulder where blood was seeping and spreading on her shirt. "Oh my God."

Maisey yanked off the pink jacket and pressed it into the wound.

Paisley hissed and her face was contorted in pain. "It's okay. I'm... fuck, it hurts."

I knelt down, looked over the wound. Winced. "That's a mess, but it looks like it went straight through."

Maisey and I looked up at the sound of cars speeding down my drive, then skidding to a stop near us.

Jed hopped from his truck, Smokey from his police SUV.

"We need an ambulance!" Maisey called. Smokey stopped his approach and spoke into his walkie talkie.

Maisey met my gaze over Paisley. "I called Jed before we came downstairs. Told him what was happening."

For the first time since the clusterfuck started, I smiled. "Woman, you're going to get your ass spanked so good for all this."

"Me?" Maisey asked, clearly appalled.

"You don't do the protecting."

"I'm the one dying here," Paisley moaned.

"You're not dying," Maisey snapped. She looked down at her sister with a scowl. "You got yourself into this mess and were shot by your own stupid partner-in-crime."

She sure as shit had. But she'd stepped in front of a bullet for her sister. And me. She might have redeemed herself. A little.

Jed squatted down beside us, took in what was going on with his usual assessing gaze. Cunningham down for the count. Paisley's wound. "Just the shoulder?"

He looked my way and I nodded.

"Looks like you've got this under control," he said. "Although, where are the rest of your clothes?"

I shook my head and rolled my eyes. "That's what you want to ask?"

"Fine. How about this: Which woman are you keeping?"

I eyed Maisey, then pointed. "That one. You'll be able to tell because she'll be the one with the very red ass."

"South!" she explained, her cheeks turning a pretty pink.

Jed chuckled. "Not a bullet wound to the shoulder?" He looked to Paisley. "Looks like your days of being identical are over."

"I can't believe you said that," Maisey continued, flustered, ignoring the sounds of pain from her sister and glaring at me.

"Right. No one sees your ass but me," I offered. I was fucking protective.

19

MAISEY

WHILE MICAH CUNNINGHAM was unconscious and needed medical attention, neither Jed nor Smokey thought he needed an ambulance to get to the hospital. It seemed, they didn't have much sympathy. I didn't either. They cuffed him while he was still out, then carried him to the back of the patrol car and loaded him up. Smokey left to get him checked out.

Since the ETA for the ambulance was over fifteen minutes, we helped Paisley into Jed's truck and he took her to the hospital instead. The second he drove around the house and disappeared, South grabbed my hand and tugged me into his studio, his foot kicking the door shut behind him. He yanked me into his arms and kissed the hell out of me. His skin was cold, but his scent surrounded me. He was so big. Thickly muscled. Yet not invincible.

I sank into him, the knowledge that Micah Cunningham was in police custody and Paisley was with Jed and on the way to the ER. That we were safe.

His tongue found mine and he devoured me. His hands tangled in my hair and he held me as he wanted me. Took the kiss from passionate to desperate.

I had no idea how long we kissed before he pulled back. We tried to catch our breaths, but I clung to him. Not wanting to ever let him go.

"Are you okay?" he breathed.

I nodded. "A little freaked still. Paisley didn't give me much time to think of some way to save you."

"Right. You saving me." He backed me up into the wall again, this time much more gently. "How many times do I have to tell you I don't need saving?"

I saw the frustration and anguish in his blue eyes. Felt it in the snug hold.

"He was going to shoot you and then blow you up!"

"You didn't know that when Paisley went upstairs to get you."

"She told me he had a gun."

"You don't have fucking Wonder Woman bracelets. You can't deflect bullets."

"Neither can you!"

And neither could Paisley, but we didn't say that. Our voices echoed off the high ceiling.

"I love you," he yelled.

"I love you, too," I yelled back.

He kissed me again. I grabbed his shirt and held on for the ride. He hoisted me up and I wrapped my legs around his waist. Felt the thick prod of his dick against my center. I whimpered, wanting him in me. Wanting more.

"I need to fuck you," he murmured, kissing along my jaw.

"Then fuck me," I said, squirming. My clit was getting some friction, but not enough. I wasn't sure if it was the adrenaline or seeing a gun waved at my man, but I needed him with a desperation I'd never felt before. "But we have to give statements to the police."

"We will."

I nodded, but I wasn't thinking too clearly since his hands were cupping my breasts.

"I have to get in you first. Now."

"Yes." I nodded again, my hands going between us to help with his jeans. He hadn't even buttoned them when he'd gone downstairs. It made for easy work for his dick to spring free.

He set me down long enough to rip my shirt open, the remaining buttons flying off. I hadn't put on a bra, so I was bare beneath. He pushed my jeans down my hips, but got frustrated when they caught on my thighs.

With hands on my shoulders, he spun me around, set my hands on the wall by my head.

"Ass out, beautiful."

I canted my hips and he spanked me.

"Stop putting yourself in danger."

"South!"

Another swat but to my other ass cheek.

"Stop trying to save me."

"I can't help it. I don't want anything to happen to you."

"We can keep arguing or we can fuck. Your call."

He didn't move and I glanced over my shoulder at him. His gaze was fixed on my butt, at the two bright pink handprints I was sure were there. He was waiting for me to answer.

"Please."

"Please what, beautiful?"

I squirmed and his hand cupped my pussy.

"You like this? Fuck, you're soaked."

"Please," I begged again.

He stepped close and thrust deep in one stroke.

"Fuck," he growled.

I cried out, arched my back. He was so big, so deep.

He wrapped an arm around me from my hip and to my opposite shoulder. I felt his chest hair against my back, and I was up on my tiptoes.

He wasn't gentle. This was fucking, pure and simple. I needed him in me, feeling him take what he wanted from my body. I needed to know he was okay, to be right there with him.

I understood why they were called quickies. I was frantic to come. Shifting my left hand, I braced myself and used my right to touch myself, circling my clit in the way I knew got me off.

"That's right," he said, leaning and nipping my shoulder. "Make yourself come."

It didn't take much until I was coming all over him. My inner walls clenched and squeezed, pulsating around him as he kept pulling back then filling me. Our bodies slapped together as I moaned my release.

"Fuck," he growled, his fingers tightening as he held himself buried inside me. Filling me with him cum.

We were breathing hard, my skin sweaty. Yet I had never felt closer to South.

"That took the edge off, but I'm never going to get rid of the picture of Cunningham pointing a gun at you," he murmured, kissing along my neck. His hold loosened and he slipped from me, then turned me to face him. He kissed me, gentle this time. "Okay?"

I nodded, meeting his blue eyes. I wasn't used to people taking care of me. I liked it. No, I loved it. I felt the wetness seeping from me, and I glanced down between us. "I think I need to clean up."

He looked too, saw his cum sliding down my thighs. "Fuck, I'm hard again."

He was.

"I didn't use a condom."

"I'm on the pill."

He nodded. "Good, then we're going bare from now on. Nothing between us, beautiful."

He tucked himself back in his jeans and went to grab a roll of paper towels from his workbench. He tore off a piece and instead of handing it to me, gently wiped my thighs and then between.

"Let's go to the hospital, deal with your sister and Cunningham."

He tossed the towel in the nearby trash can and set the roll down. Next he helped me pull my panties and jeans back up. My shirt was a lost cause; only the top two buttons remained.

"When this is all done, I'm not letting you go," he promised. "Seriously, woman. I don't care if you want to work. You're being tied to my bed until school starts in January."

I didn't argue because I really liked his idea, especially if he never put a shirt on. "Let's go and we can get to that sooner."

20

OUTH

TWO HOURS LATER, we were in the emergency room. Paisley had been put in a private room and Smokey stood outside. She was under arrest, but since she'd been shot in the shoulder and not much of a flight risk, she wasn't cuffed.

Maisey had brought her a button-up shirt the nurse had helped Paisley put on over her bandaged shoulder. Somehow, the bullet had missed anything vital or breakable. Her arm was in a sling. She'd have a tough time brushing her hair for a while, but she'd be fine in the long run. For now, she sat sideways on the gurney pumped full of pain killers. Her feet dangled, not reaching the floor.

Her face was tearstained, although I'd seen her waterworks before. I'd believed them then but was cautious now. She looked down and picked at her fingernails.

"You're going to jail," Maisey said.

She nodded, a cuticle on her thumb holding her attention. "I know." She looked up at her sister. Her eyes were a little glassy. "Unless you want to help me."

Help her? I wasn't very sympathetic, but I wasn't Maisey. I didn't have as kind of a heart. I knew what it was like to be worked over by a family member. Maisey had endured it much longer than I had. Paisley's actions hadn't just hurt her sister mentally. She'd robbed Maisey of schooling. Money she'd worked hard for. She'd stolen her life.

Macon had etched away at my confidence, but he hadn't succeeded. I'd almost fucked it up with Maisey because of it. But I was free of him now. Except Paisley had jumped in front of a bullet for us. Macon sure as shit wouldn't have done that.

That and that alone softened my feelings toward her. Barely.

I'd only press charges if Maisey did but *going to jail* meant she wasn't going to let her slide this time. I doubted the district attorney would let it slide either.

Maisey pulled her hand from my hold, took a step closer to the gurney. I glanced between the two sisters. Maisey had ditched the pink coat and replaced the flannel I'd ripped the buttons from with a navy sweater. Even though Maisey wore glasses and I knew she had my cum dripping from her and coating her panties, I could tell the differences between the two now.

Besides the bullet hole in Paisley's shoulder, they were subtle. The shape of the eyes was slightly off. Maisey held herself a little stiffer, a little more aloof. Paisley slouched even when she wasn't pumped full of pain meds. It was their... auras, their actual selves that were plain as day.

Now.

If I'd gotten closer at the bar that night I'd thought Maisey was picking up the two cowboys, I'd have noticed the differences. I just hadn't known she was a twin which meant the fucked up outcome would have been the same. Who could have imagined someone was an identical twin?

"How am I to help you?" Maisey asked.

Paisley flicked her familiar eyes at me, then back to Maisey.

"You almost had him shot and then burned in a gas explosion," she snapped. "Don't even look at him."

"Maisey," Paisley said, her name drawn out as a beg.

"Call Mom. She's helped you out of your messes before."

Paisley shrugged, then winced. "Last I heard she was in Florida with some guy she met at the casino."

From what Maisey had told me about her mother, this probably wasn't a surprise.

"You took all my money! Do you have any idea how much I needed that money?" Maisey said. Her voice wasn't a shout, but it was clear she was beyond pissed. She was shaking.

"I know. You had to stop school."

"I have a fucking lump in my breast and I didn't have money for a mammogram."

What? I blinked and almost fell back a step. "Holy fuck, woman. What?"

I turned her to face me, looked down at her chest.

"Oh my God," Paisley whispered.

"I... I found a lump and got it checked out at the free clinic. The nurse thought it was probably just a fluid filled cyst. I do too because I've read about it in my nursing books. Still, she wanted me to get a mammogram to be sure, but I didn't have the money."

"Why didn't you fucking ask me for it?" I practically shouted. I cupped her tits and started pressing and gently squeezing as if I could find it. She was soft and lush, plump and perfect, the nipples hardening beneath my palms. I loved these gorgeous mounds and I couldn't imagine something inside of one being evil. A threat.

"South!"

She swatted at my hands but I wasn't letting go until I was good and ready. "Because you didn't want to be *beholden?*" I asked.

Maisey blinked back tears and nodded. "What if it's not just a cyst? I.. I don't—"

Giving up the search, I yanked her into my arms and hugged her fiercely. I could barely breathe from the panic. "Smokey!" He stuck his head in the open doorway. "Get the doctor in here." The older man's eyes widened and glanced around concerned, but nodded and left. I didn't let her go as I heard his footsteps retreat, then hurried ones return. A nurse in blue scrubs, not a doctor, came in. She, too, looked concerned, but when no one was coding or bleeding out, she looked to me.

I pushed Maisey toward the woman. "This woman needs a mammogram. Now."

She frowned. "Sir, she's not a—"

"I'm South Wainright and I will *buy* this fucking hospital if she's not getting the procedure in the next fifteen minutes and the results from the radiologist directly after."

The woman swallowed hard. "I'll get a nurse from that department down here to escort her."

I nodded, then blew out a huge breath. "Thank you." I looked down at Maisey and cupped her cheeks. "You are in big fucking trouble."

A lump? Jesus. I'd spent time paying thorough attention to her breasts and hadn't felt anything. Then again, I was a little distracted whenever I focused on them. I had a feeling a mammogram didn't involve licking and nibbling on the nipples.

"I'm sorry," she murmured, glancing away.

I turned her chin back so I met her dark, worried eyes. "Your ass will be later," I vowed. "We deal with Paisley while we wait for the nurse, then we get your shit sorted out. Because we're going to deal with it, whatever they find."

She nodded. Not thrilled we had to even wait for the nurse, I redirected my frustration back to Paisley.

"Do you want a lawyer?" I asked her, my voice

loud. I was more riled from the lump than the attempted murder. "Someone different from the public defender?"

Paisley would be given court appointed representation, which was her right if she couldn't afford one of her own. I doubted she could. Not with the amount of shit she was in or the fact that she was a professional schemer.

"You'd do that for me?" she asked me, her eyes wide.

I shook my head. "I'd do it for Maisey."

Because Paisley had tried to protect us, I left out everything I felt about her, like how much of a selfish bitch she was. She'd gone to Mexico using money her sister needed for a fucking mammogram. Yeah, if that didn't get the woman's head on straight, I didn't know what would.

While it was clear Maisey loved her sister by how much she was consistently hurt by her, Maisey didn't *like* her. Paisley had done too much. Pushed Maisey too far.

Maybe Paisley would change in jail. I doubted it, but I wouldn't crush my woman's hope by sharing that. I grabbed Maisey's hand and kissed it. I didn't give a shit if Paisley saw my affection for her sister. Or if Jed and anyone else was watching through the open doorway.

"I didn't know he wanted to kill you," Paisley admitted, as if that would make a difference. "I tried to stop him. To protect you."

I was going to answer, but Maisey squeezed my hand. "Yeah, you did," she said. "Thank you for that. But it doesn't matter. I've dealt with the consequences of your actions all my life. You stole boyfriends from me. Money. My college tuition. This time, you almost had the man I loved killed. I'm out, Paisley."

She was more concerned about me being killed than the lump. We had to work on who was fucking protecting who. Yeah, she was going to be tied to our bed. Forever.

"I'm sorry," Paisley said, a tear sliding down her cheek.

I wasn't sure if it was an act or not. I didn't care either way.

A nurse in pink scrubs knocked on the doorframe. "Hi there! I'm Rose from the mammogram department. Wow, you two look alike. Who's headed with me?"

TWENTY MINUTES LATER, we sat in a windowless office in the radiology department. Maisey was crying.

With relief.

I wanted to cry as well because... Jesus, that had been scary.

The lump was a fluid filled cyst, just as Maisey had thought.

I'd stayed in the exam room with her when the huge machine had squished one of my favorite parts of her to a pancake. Maisey hadn't wanted me to be in there, but I'd given her a look and she let it go. Based on the pale pink walls, posters of serene landscapes and spa music being pumped from hidden speakers, this was definitely no-man's land.

Tough.

I promised the doctor Maisey would be back for follow-up imaging in six months. I also promised her I'd take responsibility for diligent breast checks from here on out. Maisey had turned as pink as the walls and the doctor couldn't help but smile. Then she left us alone and I tugged my woman onto my lap.

"What is going to get you to let me take care of you?" I asked, stroking her silky hair.

She looked up at me. Blinked.

I slid her glasses up when she said nothing. "Yeah, that's what I thought. Marry me, Maisey."

She blinked again. "Um... what?"

"Marry me." Yeah, those words felt right. I figured I'd get married someday. I hadn't played *wedding* growing up or imagined how romantic it would be when I got down on one knee. I knew I wanted to spend my life with someone, but that was it. I'd been patient, waiting for the right woman.

I'd found her.

And I asked her to marry me in the back corner of the radiology department at the local hospital.

Far from romantic that was for fucking sure. But after what we'd just went through, I wasn't wasting another second without her being mine. Without her knowing I wasn't anything without her.

She wouldn't lean on me for help until she knew, without a shadow of a doubt, that she was mine. That I wasn't going to abandon her or use her or prop her up so she fell on her face. She didn't want me for my money. That she was independent. Strong. Determined. Self-sufficient.

"You're mine," I continued. "We're a team. I want you and I want you to want me like when we didn't know each other's names. No money issues. No family problems. Nothing but you and me."

I squeezed her hip with one hand and gently cupped her breast through her shirt with the other.

"No more secrets. Your problems are mine. You don't protect me. I take care of you."

She shook her head as a shimmer of tears filled her eyes. "That's not how this works."

I nodded and flicked my thumb over her nipple. "It is. You're my heart. You take care of you, and I take care of you."

"That makes no sense."

"We live happily ever after," I added because I wasn't going to argue. She could say no, but I'd keep trying.

"South, I—"

I silenced her with a kiss.

"Marry me," I breathed.

"But—"

I kissed her again. Her lips were soft and responsive. She opened for me and fuck... yeah, she was mine.

"I know I'm tainted, got Macon's wicked blood in me," I said. "Still, marry me. Know that my money isn't to make you *beholden.* Fuck, I hate that stupid word. It makes you Mrs. South Wainright."

She cocked her head to the side. "Does that make you Mr. Maisey Miles?"

"Fuck, yes," I said as I thumbed a tear from her

cheek. If she was mine, I'd go by any name she wanted.

"Then yes."

I stared at her. "Yes?"

She laughed, flung her arms around me. "Yes!"

21

MAISEY

WHEN WE RETURNED to the ER—engaged!—all the Wainrights were there. North, West, and Jed, who I considered a Wainright. Another man, who I assumed was East, although he didn't look like his twin. My entire life would have been different if Paisley and I had been fraternal.

"Everything okay?" North asked, glancing between us. She was dressed down in jeans and a cream sweater, her hair pulled up in a sloppy bun. I had to wonder if Jed had called her and she'd dashed out of the house, skipping the high-maintenance routine she completed every day before the office.

"All good," South said, pulling me into his side as if we were going to do the three-legged race. "The lump's a fluid filled cyst. By the way, we're getting married."

North blinked. Jed eyed me as if the cyst might be an enemy and he'd have to arrest it. West and East—again, I assumed it was him—just stared.

"South!" I said, smacking him again. "They didn't need to know about the lump. God."

Good thing he didn't know the ins and outs of my period or I was sure he'd share that, too. I'd need to have a talk with him about a few boundaries before long.

"I'm... I—" North didn't know what to say. "Congratulations about both!"

She came over and hugged me. Yes, a full-on hug from North Wainright.

"Welcome to the family. I'm excited to have a sister after being stuck with these three morons. You can tell me about these cysts and I won't blab about them like South. Girl talk. I hear it's a thing."

"I'd... I'd like that."

West hugged me next. "Nice job," he murmured.

"I'm East, by the way," East said, tilting his head to

South. "No manners. Maybe you can teach this caveman some."

"She likes when I'm a caveman," South added. He pushed on East's arm. "Stop hugging my woman."

I couldn't help but laugh. This joking, the silliness, was what I imagined families to really be like.

Jed gave me a smile—an actual Jed Barnett smile! —and a wink.

"I'm glad your sister is okay," North said. I knew we had to talk about the elephant in the room. My crazy sister and South's insane half-brother.

"She jumped in front of a bullet for us," I said.

"Jed told me about the evil twin," East told me. "Although the taking-a-bullet thing might make her a little less evil. Either way, I had to come see for myself." He tipped his head toward West. "If there's any doubt, between us, he's the evil twin."

West rubbed his hands together. "Sounds fun."

"I'm also here to make sure you and South are both okay."

"It's good to see your face," South told him. "Just so you know, staying with me this year for the holidays is out."

East laughed and thumbed toward West. "I'll stay at the bachelor pad."

The Wainrights glanced over my shoulder. I

turned to see a deputy escorted Paisley out of the exam room.

Paisley stopped and offered me a small smile. Her hair was snarled. Her shirt was buttoned incorrectly and the bulky bandage on her shoulder made it hang funny. Her face was streaked with makeup and spots of blood. There was none of the confidence and swagger she always had. She looked... defeated. Maybe, finally, the impact of her actions was obvious to her. "What did the doctor say?" she asked me, her brow puckered with concern.

"All good," I told her.

Paisley smiled for real this time. "Good. For what it's worth, I'm sorry."

I didn't say anything. I couldn't. Maybe someday I'd forgive her. Time would tell. For now, I was content knowing she'd be finally facing the consequences of her actions.

Smokey led her past us to the exit, the doors opening and sliding closed silently behind them.

South pulled me close once again and kissed the top of my head. I knew now that I wasn't alone, that I was loved, and I had a feeling South was going to remind me of it every chance he had.

"What about Cunningham?" South asked.

Jed pointed toward a second exam room. The door

was open and it had a window so the patient could be seen from the nurses station. He was lying on a gurney and a police officer was posted to keep watch. Most of the blood on his face had been washed away, but his nose had been set, bandages in place, and the rest of his face was swollen. Unlike Paisley, he was cuffed to the metal bed frame. He looked awful, and I didn't care at all. He'd planned to kill South. I didn't even want to think about the pervy stuff he'd planned for me *and* my sister.

Just looking at him made me understand South's protective instincts because I felt a hell of a lot of protectiveness for him in return. I wanted to go into that room and beat the crap out of Micah even though South had done a pretty good job.

"He's going down for attempted murder," Jed said.

When I'd first met him in July cleaning the house, he'd been so serious. I've watched as North lightened him up a bit and he smiled often, usually just for her. Right now, he was his usual grim self as his gaze was fixed on Micah Cunningham.

"Who the hell is this guy again?" East asked, rubbing a hand over a short beard.

A doctor passed us and she wrote something on a huge dry erase board on the wall.

Jed handed East a few sheets of paper. East began

scanning them as Jed spoke. "Micah Cunningham. Thirty-three. We don't have DNA proof... yet, but he says he's Macon's son. I guess before Macon met your mother, he met Ruth Cunningham."

"They dated?" East asked, eyes wide. "I thought he was gay."

West shrugged, stuffed his hands in his jean's pockets. He must've come right off the range because he was dusty and smelled faintly of oil and engine exhaust. "We don't know their relationship other than they supposedly fucked once and sperm met egg and made Micah."

Jed nodded and East frowned.

"What?" West asked. "I read the printout before you got here."

A phone rang behind us.

"Then we ask Ruth what happened," East added. "Or why she didn't give Micah Macon's last name."

"She's dead," South said, remembering what Cunningham had said in my house.

"What is it with everyone being dead?" East asked, crossing his arms over his chest. "Why can't there be someone still alive who knows what the hell went on back then?"

No one had an answer to that.

"It would be a hell of a lot easier to figure out the

truth if Ruth Cunningham was alive. Same goes with mom," South continued. "I wanted to know why she had sex with Macon if he wasn't into her, or any woman. Then there's mom. Why be with Macon if she had North with a mystery man before me and East and West with the same guy after?"

Right. South had said that while they shared a mother, he was the only one with Macon as a father. I didn't remember him mentioning that North and the twins had the same father. It was really confusing.

No one had an answer, and I was just catching on to the complexity of their family and just how awful Macon Wainright was.

"Once he's released from medical care, Smokey will take Cunningham to jail," Jed said. "He won't get bail."

Good. He was completely unstable.

"Would he still be able to get Macon's money?" North asked.

Jed looked at her and his expression softened. "If he's Macon's heir, then yes."

That made me so mad. While I understood why South didn't want his father's money—the father who he seemed to hate more than anyone—it made no sense why a guy who'd murder his own brother for *that* money should get any of it.

"I... I donated it," North began, then looked to South, a worried look in her eye. "All of it, like you wanted."

"That's good," South said, offering her a reassuring smile. "Macon's probably rolling over in his grave, but I finally won one against the bastard."

"Will that make problems?" she asked, looking to her brothers. "With Cunningham?"

"Shit, is he going to sue?" East wondered.

Jed shrugged. "The payment was made before he was officially identified as an heir. That's *if* he really is one. A nurse took a DNA sample, so we'll know soon. If he's telling the truth, I guess he could take it to court, but he'll have to do it from prison."

"What if there are others?" East asked as a tech pushed a medical cart past us.

"Other half-siblings?" South wondered. "As long as they don't want me dead, I'd like to meet them. They can even come to our wedding." South laced his fingers with mine. "Come on, beautiful. I need you all to myself for a while."

22

MAISEY

"YOUR ASS WAS the first thing I saw when I met you."

I popped up, stared at South over the fridge door.

We weren't at Billionaire Ranch, but his farmhouse, yet he was leaning against a doorway just as he had that day. Had it been less than a week? His look was just as eager, just as intense now.

I knew more. Knew South. Knew love. In such a short time, my world changed. Flipped.

I smiled. "Ham or roast beef?"

He pushed off the wall and came to me. "I'll give you some beef."

I couldn't help but laugh, but when I glanced at him, he wasn't. I set the cold cuts on the counter and closed the door.

South didn't look away. Veer. Blink.

"I thought you were hungry?" I asked, licking my lips. I wasn't afraid of him and I certainly wasn't going to deny him kisses or anything else. I was still surprised by his intensity, especially since it was focused solely and completely on me.

We'd returned from the hospital a little while ago. South had wanted to clean up the blood in front of his studio. I figured his efforts were more for me—so I didn't see the reminder of what had happened—than anything since the snow that would be coming overnight would probably wash it away. However, I had a feeling he'd do anything to make the horrors of the day disappear and I wasn't going to deny him that opportunity. While he'd done that, I'd cleaned up the dust and pieces of his living room ceiling that had fallen to the floor when Micah Cunningham shot it, then set about making us some lunch. Besides a little ceiling patchwork near the fireplace, it was as if it hadn't happened.

But it had and it was going to stick with both of us.

"I am hungry," he said, moving toward me. I held my ground, but he didn't slow, only leaned down and tossed me over his shoulder. "For you. Your pussy. *My* pussy."

"South!"

He took the stairs at a quick pace and spanked my ass on the way. "After you have your punishment."

Before I could ask him what he meant, he dropped me on the bed. Dropped, like a sack of potatoes. No ladylike landing for me. I was all elbows and bent legs.

"Punishment?" I asked as I struggled to my knees.

"I seem to keep reminding you that you need to stop protecting me. A red ass might help."

"Then you need one too for thinking you're tainted," I countered.

His eyes narrowed and he crossed his arms over his chest. Yeah, his dick was hard in his jeans and this wasn't going the way he wanted, but... tough.

"I remember what you said at the hospital." I came up onto my knees and pulled his hands down. "You saw what my sister is capable of. Do you think I'm tainted because we're family?"

He looked at me like I was crazy. "Hell, no."

"We look exactly alike. I mean, Paisley and I even share the same DNA. How much more alike can two people get, and yet you don't think I'm tainted?"

He frowned because he'd been caught in his own logic. He couldn't even counter because my example was really fucking good. Macon was only his father where my sister and I were scientifically identical.

"Macon was... awful," he said, his shoulders slumping.

"Then you know exactly how you *don't* want to be. When we have kids, they'll never know him or what he was like because you'll be such an amazing father."

"Kids?" he asked, his eyes widening. "You want kids? Shit, between my genes and yours, we're bound to have twins."

"You're right, but that's not the point. You're not tainted, South Wainright."

"You saw my half-brother."

"He may not be related," I reminded. "Even if he *is* related, it's through your dad."

"Exactly!"

I cupped his cheeks. Felt the heat of his skin, the rasp of his whiskers. "From what you told me, your mother loved you and your siblings. She was kind and generous. Like you. You take after her, not your father."

"Still..."

I undid his belt buckle as I asked, "Do you want me to repeat what I told you about me and Paisley?"

"No." His gaze dropped to my hands now on the button of his jeans. I slid down the zipper then pushed his pants and boxers low on his hips. His dick sprang free, all hard and ready for me.

"Do you want me to stop?" I asked. "We can keep arguing."

"Fuck no."

I gripped the base and gave it one pump. Leaning down, I licked at the bead of pre-cum at the tip. "Do you want me to stop now?"

"Beautiful," he murmured.

"Yes?" I asked, looking up at him with innocent eyes, although I felt anything but.

When his fingers tangled in my hair and gently pulled me forward, I felt powerful.

"Be a good girl and suck me down."

I liked being a good girl, especially for him, so I opened wide and took as much of him as I could. I'd never done this before. Never initiated either. But I needed him.

To feel alive. To feel as connected to him as possible.

"I've never seen anything hotter in my life. You taking my dick like that."

I glanced up at him through my lashes, sucking and licking the satiny skin, yet almost gagging on how big and hard he was. I'd never done this before—

South had yet to let me take any kind of control—and hoped I was doing it right.

His head fell back, and his eyes closed. He swore and growled as I worked him. The way his hips rocked toward me; I had a feeling he liked it. Then he pulled me back and I popped off.

"Fuck, that was incredible. I'm not finishing in your mouth... this time. Clothes off, beautiful."

I shed them as fast as I could as he toed off his boots and stripped with just as much haste.

He cupped my breasts again. "They sore from that mean machine?"

I shook my head. Even though the lump had been in one, they'd done imagery for both. I'd gotten the all-clear but they were now a fascination of South's.

"I'm checking these beauties. Every day," he promised, gently kneading them.

I wasn't going to argue because I liked his way of *checking*. My nipples were hard and very sensitive as he plucked and pinched them.

He pushed me and I fell onto my back and he followed, propped up on his forearms over me. I moved my legs so he settled between my thighs. His dick was nestled at my entrance.

"I knew it the first time I saw you, Maisey Miles,"

he whispered. "You're the one for me. You. Not Paisley."

He pushed into me in one long stroke. I gasped and shifted, adjusting to his size. I wondered if I'd ever get used to taking all of him.

"I... I knew it the first time I saw you, Hot Cowboy," I replied. "You're the one for me. You. Not your billions."

He tossed his head back and laughed and I joined in. When it made my inner walls clench around him, he growled.

"Fuck, beautiful."

"Yes, please. Now. Hard."

"As you wish." He settled down to his task. Hard. Thorough. And all mine.

———

Ready for more Billionaire Ranch?
Turn to East now!

BONUS CONTENT

Guess what? I've got some bonus content for you! Sign up for my mailing list. There will be special bonus content for some of my books, just for my subscribers. Signing up will let you hear about my next release as soon as it is out, too (and you get a free book...wow!)

As always...thanks for loving my books and the wild ride!

JOIN THE WAGON TRAIN!

If you're on Facebook, please join my closed group, the Wagon Train! Don't miss out on the giveaways and hot cowboys!

https://www.facebook.com/ groups/vanessavalewagontrain/

GET A FREE BOOK!

Join my mailing list to be the first to know of new releases, free books, special prices and other author giveaways.

http://freeromanceread.com

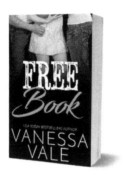

ALSO BY VANESSA VALE

For the most up-to-date listing of my books:

vanessavalebooks.com

All Vanessa Vale titles are available at Apple, Google, Kobo, Barnes & Noble, Amazon and other retailers worldwide.

ABOUT VANESSA VALE

Vanessa Vale is the *USA Today* bestselling author of sexy romance novels, including her popular Bridgewater historical series and hot contemporary romances. With over one million books sold, Vanessa writes about unapologetic bad boys who don't just fall in love, they fall hard. Her books are available worldwide in multiple languages in e-book, print, audio and even as an online game. When she's not writing, Vanessa savors the insanity of raising two boys and figuring out how many meals she can make with a pressure cooker. While she's not as skilled at social media as her kids, she loves to interact with readers.

Made in the USA
Columbia, SC
02 December 2021

50006752R00130